"No matter how hard things got those last few months here, you were still my wife. We were still the Starks."

She almost gasped, and he wasn't sure if she was touched or shocked or what. Part of him felt as though he knew her inside out. But he'd lost two years. And now he felt he didn't know her at all. She'd "buried" her husband. She'd raised quadruplet babies on her own for a year. She was obviously strong in ways he hadn't been here to witness.

Was she still his wife? Could they pick up where they'd left off—even if things between them had been rocky? Or, given how troubled their marriage had been then and all the time that had passed—not to mention the big lie of his death—was it just too late for them?

He sure hoped not.

* * *

THE WYOMING MULTIPLES:
Lots of babies, lots of love

Dear Reader,

Second chances are so rare. This Christmas, though, a mom of baby quadruplets will discover that her police sergeant husband, supposedly killed in the line of duty two years ago, faked his death to protect her. Now Theo Stark is back in Wedlock Creek, Wyoming, no idea he's a father of four little ones...

Before, Theo's job came first and he was reluctant to start a family. Their marriage was seriously rocky. Now Allie wonders if her husband's heart is truly with his newfound family or if he's back out of obligation. Both Mr. and Mrs. Stark—and their marriage—have been given that rare second chance. And this time around, it's not just the two of them.

I hope you enjoy Allie and Theo's second-chance love story! I love to hear from readers. Feel free to visit my website and write me at MelissaSenate@yahoo.com.

Warm regards and all my wishes for a happy holiday season,

Melissa Senate

Wyoming Christmas Surprise

Melissa Senate

Recycling programs for this product may not exist in your area.

ISBN-13: 978-1-335-46612-9

Wyoming Christmas Surprise

This edition published by arrangement with Harlequin Books S.A.

For questions and comments about the quality of this book, please contact us at CustomerService@Harlequin.com.

Printed in U.S.A.

Melissa Senate has written many novels for Harlequin and other publishers, including her debut, *See Jane Date*, which was made into a TV movie. She also wrote seven books for Harlequin's Special Edition line under the pen name Meg Maxwell. Her novels have been published in over twenty-five countries. Melissa lives on the coast of Maine with her teenage son; their rescue shepherd mix, Flash; and a lap cat named Cleo. For more information, please visit her website, melissasenate.com.

Books by Melissa Senate

Harlequin Special Edition

The Wyoming Multiples

Detective Barelli's Legendary Triplets
The Baby Switch!

***Hurley's Homestyle Kitchen* (as Meg Maxwell)**

Santa's Seven-Day Baby Tutorial
Charm School for Cowboys
The Cook's Secret Ingredient
The Cowboy's Big Family Tree
The Detective's 8 lb, 10 oz Surprise
A Cowboy in the Kitchen

Montana Mavericks: The Lonelyhearts Ranch

The Maverick's Baby in Waiting

***Montana Mavericks: The Great Family Roundup* (as Meg Maxwell)**

Mommy and the Maverick

Red Dress Ink

Questions to Ask Before Marrying
Love You to Death
See Jane Date

Dedicated to my son, Max—truly sweet sixteen.

Chapter One

"Something old, something new, something borrowed, something blue."

Bride-to-be Allie MacDougal Stark stood in front of the mirror in the Wedlock Creek Town Hall's "Bridal Preparation" room, her sisters, Lila and Merry, on either side of her. Lila, the most traditional of the MacDougal triplets, was insisting that Allie tick off the old wedding poem checklist.

Even though nothing about today's wedding was traditional.

"Hmm, something old," Lila said, tilting her head and surveying Allie's reflection. "Ah—got it. You're wearing Grandma's pearl drop earrings. Perfect."

The earrings were beautiful, and Allie loved the idea

of having a part of her beloved grandmother with her today.

"And the 'something borrowed' are my shoes," Merry pointed out, gesturing at the salmon-colored suede pumps on Allie's feet. They were a great match for the blush-colored lace jacket and matching knee-length pencil skirt that Allie wore for every special occasion. The usual shoes that went with this outfit had horribly scuffed heels, so Merry and her shoe collection to the rescue.

"Something new is next," Lila said. "Sexy underthings perhaps?" she added, wriggling her blond eyebrows.

Uh, no. Allie made a face at her sister, who knew perfectly well that things between her and her fiancé didn't—and would likely never—merit a trip to Victoria's Secret. Honestly, if tonight, their wedding night, she and Elliot watched a movie and played Boggle before turning in early with a peck on the cheek, she wouldn't be surprised.

"You know," Allie said, looking herself up and down, "I don't think I have *anything* new on right now."

As if she would. As the widowed mother of eleven-month-old quadruplets, *new* was not a word in Allie's vocabulary. She hadn't bought anything for herself in at least two years, and most of the quads' stuff—and there was a lot of stuff—was hand-me-downs or gifts.

"You actually *do* have something new, though," Merry said, nodding at Lila, who ran over to her purse on the chair in the corner and pulled out a small square box.

"What is this?" Allie asked as Lila handed it to her.

Merry smiled. "Open it. It's your wedding present from us."

"You guys," Allie said, looking from one sister to the other and back to the box. She opened the lid. Aww—it was a beautiful oval-shaped gold locket on a filigree chain.

"Now open the locket," Lila said.

Allie flicked open the tiny latch. An itty-bitty photo of her babies, one she recognized was taken just a few weeks ago, was nestled inside. Tyler and Henry were smiling, Ethan was midlaugh, and Olivia had her big toe in her mouth, her trademark move.

Her heart squeezed. Her sisters were *everything*. "I love it," Allie said, grabbing each MacDougal in a hug. "I absolutely love it. But I have to say I'm surprised you got me anything."

Her sisters had made their feelings about her marriage to Elliot Talley crystal clear. *Don't marry a man you're not in love with*, Lila had said quite a few times. *You have us!* Merry had insisted even last night, when the triplets had gotten together for a "bachelorette party," which meant dinner at Allie's favorite restaurant for incredible Mexican food and margaritas. *We'll always help you with the kiddos*, Lila had said. *You don't* have *to do this.*

This was marrying Elliot Talley in about twenty minutes.

"Of course we did," Lila said. "Because we love you and support you." She took the necklace out of the box and put it around Allie's neck. "I can never fasten these things," she said, frowning. "I have fat fingers."

Merry laughed and took over. “We all have the same fingers. And mine are *not* fat.”

Allie snorted. “Mine, either,” she said, wiggling hers in the air. The Irish friendship ring Elliot had given her as a symbol of their commitment when he’d proposed barely gleamed in the bright room. Lila wrinkled her nose at it. *Hardly traditional*, she’d groused the day Allie, newly engaged, had shown it to her sisters.

Allie didn’t need or want a diamond ring. She had one, the beautiful solitaire in a gold band that her late husband had given her six months before they’d married seven years ago. After Elliot had proposed, she’d moved the diamond ring and wedding band to her right hand, but they didn’t fit comfortably on any of her fingers. So she’d put them away, dropping to her knees afterward in a round of sobs that had shaken her entire body.

“Wait, what about something blue?” Lila said, shoving her long, curly blond hair behind her shoulders. “You don’t have anything blue.”

Blue. The face of police sergeant Theo Stark, killed almost two years ago in the line of duty, was vivid in her mind, the first time she saw him in uniform as a twenty-four-year-old cadet in the police academy. He’d joined right after three tours of duty in the army.

“Sure I do,” Allie said, sucking in a breath. “A twofold ‘something blue.’ Theo’s memory. With me always.”

Lila’s face crumpled. “Oh, God, now I’m gonna cry.”

“Me, too,” Merry said and squeezed Allie in a hug, Lila smushing her way in.

“You’ll ruin your mascara,” Lila warned, stepping back and handing Allie a tissue. “You can’t marry Elliot with raccoon tracks down your face.”

Merry opened her mouth to say something, then turned away and put on her usual pleasant expression, and Allie knew exactly what her sister had wanted to say.

You can't marry Elliot, period.

Allie had been dating Elliot, a kind, responsible tax accountant, for only three months. According to her sisters, *dating* was a stretch, considering they'd never had sex. Ten years her senior at forty-one, Elliot wanted a family, she had a ready-made one, and they got along great. Their relationship had the added bonus of increasing his business, since he seemed like a saint to everyone in Wedlock Creek, and the proposal had turned him into a hometown hero.

People felt bad for Allie Stark, widowed mother of baby quadruplets. For the first few months after they were born, she'd barely had to lift one baby, let alone figure out how to juggle four. Her family, neighbors, even total strangers in town had rallied around her, whispers of "that poor woman," "those poor babies," wherever she went with her huge choo-choo train of a four-seat stroller. Her freezer was still stocked with everything from casseroles to soups. She had an entire kitchen drawer full of gift cards to Baby Blitz. And babysitting offers, from overnights to a few hours to let her nap and pee and have a cup of coffee, had been aplenty. But six months in, Allie had known she had to start standing on her own two feet and learn how to take care of her children by herself.

Her sisters had been pushing her to date, to get back out there, but even if she could imagine being with another man, there had been no takers. Not one. Not a surprise, considering she came with four babies. So three months ago, when Elliot asked her out, she'd been so surprised and actually kind of touched and had said yes. He was something of a homebody, enjoying staying in and cooking interesting pasta dishes and playing with the babies. He thoughtfully bought them teething rings and chew books that could be read in the bathtub. He also hadn't pushed her for sex, which she appreciated given her exhaustion. He'd said they'd move their relationship to that level when she was ready—and that if she were never ready, that would be fine, too. Allie had a few theories about Elliot's lack of a sex drive where she was concerned, but when it came right down to it, she was in this for security for her children.

Her sisters did understand—anyone would understand—why she'd said yes to a lack of passion for a sense of security and a father for the quads. Allie did care for Elliot and she *did* want a father for the babies, someone she could trust, someone she could count on. And Elliot, as tax-accountant-desk-job-safe as Theo had been cop-on-the-street-dangerous, would never make her worry in that way she always had. And so she'd said yes. She'd finally accepted that Theo Stark, her husband of five years until she'd lost him and any hope of saving their rocky marriage two years ago, was gone. That acceptance had taken almost everything out of her.

And this wedding was what it was, so Allie hadn't booked the famed and beautiful Wedlock Creek Wedding Chapel, which attracted couples from all over the country. According to legend, those who married in the century-old chapel would have multiples in some way, shape or form, à la twins or triplets or quadruplets or more, through luck, science or pure happenstance. Allie's late parents had married at the chapel thirty-two years ago and had triplet daughters. Allie had married at the chapel and had quadruplets—three boys and a girl.

The town hall, with its fluorescent lighting and drab interior, was a far cry from the chapel, with its heart-shaped bell atop the steeple, gorgeous stained glass windows and gingerbread tiers that resembled a Victorian wedding cake. One hundred sixty-two guests had gathered to watch her and Theo say their vows in the famed chapel. Today, it would be just her and Elliot, and two witnesses—the town clerk and the receptionist. Her sisters had popped in to wish her luck—and to give her the gift, apparently. Then they were going back to Allie's house to babysit the quads, who were being treated to lunch by Allie's neighbor, a wonderful grandmother of fourteen who'd raised quintuplets and had lived to tell the tale. She, too, had married at the chapel.

"Okay, we're gonna head back," Merry said. "We'll see you at home around two."

Allie nodded. The plan was for her and Elliot to treat themselves to a decadent lunch at Marcello's, a great Italian restaurant here in town, and then go back to Allie's house to jump right into life as the married parents of eleven-month-old quadruplets. No honeymoon this time around. Seven years ago, she and Theo had flown to Paris, staying only for a weekend, since they couldn't afford much back then, and it was all the honeymoon she needed for a lifetime.

Her sisters gave her one final hug each, then headed for the door.

Allie stared at her reflection in the mirror and

smoothed her special-occasion suit, thinking back to the stunning white strapless gown with intricate beading and just enough bling to make her feel like a princess. *Whatevs*, she thought. *This suit makes me feel like an adult.*

"Oh, one more thing, Allie," Lila said at the door, with her trademark devilish grin. "Just promise me one thing."

"What's that?" Allie asked, eyebrow raised.

Lila put a hand over her heart. "Promise me. Us. Yourself—that you're not going to change your name. You can't be Allie Talley. You can't *rhyme*."

Merry let out a snort, then gave Lila a jab in the ribs.

Allie laughed. "Well, if I do change my name and become Allie Talley, at least it'll make me laugh."

Merry grabbed a giggling Lila out the door. Leaving Allie to stare at herself in the mirror, wondering what it was going to feel like to be Allie Talley, who that woman was. She had been Allie Stark for the past seven years—five as his wife, two as his widow. But life had a way of throwing monkey wrenches and curveballs and all sorts of shocks and surprises at people. You had to adapt, change the plan to fit the new now.

You're the new you, a grief counselor had said at the bereavement group she'd attended for a few months. She hadn't mentioned that to her sisters, that she herself was the "something new" for today; her reason for keeping it to herself had stolen her breath.

Because she'd give anything for her old imperfect life back, a second chance.

But she was "the new her," so in twenty minutes she was marrying Elliot and becoming Allie Talley.

Allie Talley. She smiled, thinking of Lila, and a small laugh came out of her. She'd been about to make herself cry, but becoming the new her, becoming the rhyme of Allie Talley, had lightened the mood.

Badumpa.

Everything is going to be okay, she told herself. She picked up the locket from where it lay just under the V of her jacket and flicked open the latch. Tyler, Henry, Ethan, Olivia. Everything she did, she did for them.

But suddenly all she wanted to do was race out the door after her sisters.

I'm alive.

I'm not dead.

Scratch that—that'll be obvious the second she sees you.

I had to fake my death.

I've been walking, talking, breathing, living on this earth all this time...

Sunglasses on, Stetson pulled down low, Theo Stark sat in a booth in the truck stop diner just outside the town limits of Wedlock Creek, waiting for a refill of his coffee and practicing in his head what he was going to say to Allie when he finally saw her again.

For the first time in almost two years.

On the drive up from southern Wyoming, he'd replayed what he'd say over and over. But the closer he got to Wedlock Creek, the more none of it sounded right. It was all the truth, of course, but when it came right down to it, his wife believed he was dead. And he wasn't.

At first, he wouldn't have to say anything. The fact that he was alive would be obvious.

God.

At just after one forty-five this morning, he'd gotten the call that had finally brought him back to life. The serial killer who'd turned Theo's world upside down was now dead. The threat was gone.

And Theo could come out of the shadows.

Last year at this time, with the weeks counting down to the holidays, he'd wanted nothing more than to get that call so he could go home for Christmas. He'd been hiding out for months at that point, alive and well on a remote cattle ranch, when everyone believed he was dead. Living under a fake name, keeping to himself, earning just enough to get by and move on if necessary. But the months went on and on until, finally, the call he'd been waiting for had come. He was going home.

The waitress came over with the refill, and Theo ducked his head low, nodding a thank-you. He'd recognized the woman, who used to work in the coffee shop on Main Street. But he couldn't risk anyone recognizing *him* and gasping. Since he was supposed to be dead, he figured anyone who did a double take would assume he was just a guy who looked a lot like the Wedlock Creek police sergeant who'd been killed in the line of duty. But he wasn't taking any chances until he explained himself to Allie.

While the waitress poured, making small talk about the weather, he reached for the *Wedlock Creek Chatter* the previous customer had left on the table and pretended great interest in flipping through the free weekly newspaper. Anything to keep his head down and conversation to the bare minimum. The waitress left and he breathed a sigh of relief.

He was about to push the newspaper aside when a small boxed notice on the People in the News page caught his eye. His heart started to pound and he read the two-line notice again.

Then again.

Today was Thursday. And it was now, according to the clock on the wall, 11:40 am.

Theo threw a ten-dollar bill on the table, shot out of the booth and the diner, and jumped into his black pickup, a trail of dust in his wake as he sped toward town.

Toward Allie. His wife. About to marry another man.

No. No, no, no, no.

He had twenty minutes to stop her. He was fifteen minutes from the town hall. A five-year veteran of the Wedlock Creek Police Department, the former sergeant knew full well that a patrol car would be hidden in the alley just after East Elm Road; people loved to speed on the service road into the center of town. And though Theo wanted to floor the gas pedal, he couldn't risk getting pulled over.

Because no one, except for one FBI agent and one US marshal, knew that he was alive, that he hadn't been killed in an explosion during a stakeout gone terribly wrong.

He'd pay a visit to his captain later. The first person who deserved the truth about him was Allie. He'd explain and—

And what? he thought, gripping the steering wheel. She'd moved on. She was marrying someone else.

Maybe he should let her. Allie deserved love and happiness. She deserved a good life with whoever this

Elliot Talley was. An accountant. Accountants didn't risk their lives. They didn't get shot at by bad guys. They didn't almost get blown up in dark old supposedly abandoned buildings.

Or fake their deaths.

Thing was, regardless of all that, Allie was already married.

So he had a wedding to stop. That was all he knew for sure right now.

He pulled into a parking spot in the back lot at the town hall and rushed inside, taking the stairs two at a time. A gold plaque marked Ceremonies was on the door at the far end of the long hallway. Theo sucked in a breath and pulled open the door, ready to shout *Stop the wedding!* like an insane person, but there were two people standing in front of a podium behind the mayor of Wedlock Creek and neither of them was Allie.

They—and the mayor officiating—swiveled their heads toward the door, expressions annoyed at the intrusion.

"Sorry," he said, ducking back out.

Phew. Or then again, maybe he was too late. Maybe they were ahead of schedule.

Next to the Ceremonies room was a door with another plaque: Bridal Preparation.

As Theo stood there, staring at the door, pushing his hat down even lower on his head as two people walked past, he realized Allie was in that Bridal Preparation room. He *felt* it. He felt *her.*

She was in there.

Allie. His wife.

He sucked in another breath and thought about taking off the sunglasses and the hat, but there were people walking at the other end of the hallway. People he recognized.

The black-and-white utilitarian clock on the wall said it was eleven fifty-six. There was no time to figure out what to say, how to say it.

He knocked.

As the door opened, Allie, beautiful Allie, was smiling and saying something about needing help with a tie.

She'd been expecting her groom, he figured.

But then she saw him and froze and her smile faded.

And she whispered his name.

"Theo."

Chapter Two

Allie had been freshening her lipstick when someone knocked on the door. She'd glanced at the clock. Eleven fifty-six. She'd figured it was Elliot needing help with his tie. He always dressed for their dates in a sports jacket and tie—and the tie was always either crooked or the knot halfway down his shirt. She'd opened the door, expecting to see Elliot's kind, pale face in the doorway.

But it wasn't Elliot.

It was a ghost.

Theo. Wearing dark sunglasses and a black Stetson pulled down low. Even so, she recognized him. *Knew* it was him.

It can't really be Theo, Allie thought numbly, her head spinning, her knees wobbly. *I'm dreaming. I'm hallucinating.*

"Theo," she whispered. "Theo."

He took off the hat and held it against his chest, then pocketed the sunglasses in his black leather jacket.

She gasped at how real he looked. Same thick dark hair, same intense green eyes, same scar along his chiseled jawline. Very tall at six foot two. Muscular, as always. Were ghosts muscular? Of course not.

You're seeing things, she told herself, staring at him, aware her mouth was hanging open, as she reached out like a crazy person to touch him. *He's not here. He died almost two years ago.*

His ghost had come to tell her not to marry Elliot Talley, a man she didn't love "that way," she figured. Or his ghost was here to give his blessing. One or the other.

"It's me," Theo said, reaching out a hand to touch the side of her face. "Oh, God, Allie. It is so good to see you. I have so much to tell you."

The contact of his hand on her face was real. *He* was real.

"It's so good to see me?" she sputtered. "What?" She shook her head again, sure he wouldn't still be there. "I was at your funeral. You're..."

He stepped inside the room and shut the door, then took both her hands and led her over to the two chairs by the mirror. She sat down right before her legs gave out. "I didn't die that night, Allie. Obviously," he added in a choked voice as he sat beside her. "But I had to make everyone think I did to protect you."

She slowly shook her head again, trying to listen as he started saying something about the serial killer he and his team had been after for months. "He threatened—"

A knock on the door interrupted him.

"Um, Allie?" called the voice of Elliot Talley. Her fiancé. The man she was supposed to marry in two minutes. "I need to talk to you."

She glanced at Theo, who moved against the wall. He put back on the dark sunglasses.

"Allie?" Elliot called out again with another knock. "I really have to talk to you."

Well, Elliot, she thought as she stood up, legs like rubber, *it's kind of perfect timing, since I have to talk to you, too. Seems marrying you would make me a bigamist.* There went her knees again, wobbling around.

She pulled open the door. Now it *was* Elliot who stood in the doorway, looking pale as the ghost she'd thought Theo was a minute ago. Elliot looked sick, his face a bit contorted in pain, one hand clutching his stomach.

"Allie. Oh, God, Allie. I can't do this. I'm sorry," Elliot said. "I thought I could do it, but I can't. I'm sorry. One baby, sure. But—" He shook his head. "I'm sorry. Maybe this is just cold feet and I'll come to my senses later, but I don't think so. I'm so sorry." He reached for her hand and squeezed it, then turned and ran down the hall. Allie stared after him openmouthed until he pushed through the door of the town hall.

Well, she thought.

"That him, running through the parking lot?" Theo asked, gesturing out the window.

Allie walked over to the window, more aware of her husband standing beside her, the presence of him, than of her runaway groom, racing to his car in his tan suit. They watched as he got into his car and peeled out.

Allie sank back down onto a chair. She'd been

so careful not to sit and wrinkle her outfit. Now she planned to ball this suit up and chuck it. Or give it to Goodwill.

Theo was alive? Theo was alive. Theo was *alive*.

She couldn't think, couldn't process.

"How did you even know to come here?" she asked, barely able to get the words out.

Because he's been keeping tabs on you, she figured. It was the only thing that made sense. He couldn't let her get married when she already had a husband—alive and well. So he'd rushed over to stop the wedding.

If anyone has any reason why these two should not be husband and wife, speak now or forever hold your peace.

Then again, did mayors officiating even say that at town hall weddings? She wasn't sure.

I object! she imagined Theo calling out, rushing in at the last possible second. *Turns out I'm not dead!*

She was losing her mind. Obviously. Her dead husband, whose funeral she had attended, was sitting right beside her, and she was out of her mind. She couldn't think straight, couldn't think.

Did the entire police department know the truth? Had they been informing him what was going on in her life? Was that why he'd turned up here at the last possible second?

No, she realized suddenly.

No one was keeping tabs on her for him. She knew that with certainty. Because even if he was able to leave her, to stay "buried" for two years, there was no way he would have stayed away if he'd known about the quadruplets. She knew next to nothing about what had led Theo to fake his death, but she knew *him*.

Oh, God. He didn't know he was a father. He had no idea.

Her brain was moving a mile a minute—so many questions, assumptions. And then her mind just shut down and filled with static and, inexplicably, the wedding march. She heard it playing over and over. Her brain on overload.

She shook her head again, trying to make some sense of this. Theo was here. Alive.

He pulled something from the pocket of his jacket, a folded-up piece of newspaper. He unfolded it and pointed.

Ah. It was the wedding announcement her sisters had insisted on placing, since Allie had said no to anything wedding-ish. She'd relented on the announcement mostly to quash the whispers she still heard in the supermarket and at the baby/toddler play center: *There's that poor widow with the quadruplets! Look, she has two different sneakers on and Cheerios in her hair.* She'd figured that literally alerting the media to her impending nuptials would stop the pity.

She could imagine what people would be whispering now. *Turns out her husband wasn't dead after all, and she had no idea! That poor not-a-widow!*

Theo looked down at the floor for a moment, then back up at her. "You know that truck stop diner on the freeway about ten minutes out of town?"

Of course she knew it. They'd gotten gas there a zillion times over their five years together. Early on in their marriage, when they'd stay up all night just talking, they'd go to the twenty-four-hour diner at two thirty in the morning for omelets and home fries, gazing at each other like lovesick dopes. It was just a greasy spoon, but they made amazing chocolate milkshakes and the Starks had gone at least twice a week. Of course, that was years ago. Before, before, before.

"Well, I stopped in to fill up the truck," he said, "and then I figured I'd have a few cups of coffee to prepare myself, to figure out what I was going to say, how I was going to just knock on your door and tell you I was alive. I'd gone over all that in my mind during the five-hour drive to Wedlock Creek, but as I got so close, everything went out of my head. All I could think about was the look that would be on your face. How I'd lied and betrayed you. I could barely move from the booth. Until I saw the wedding announcement."

She stood up and moved to the window. "If you say you did it to protect me, I believe you, Theo."

But something was poking at her—at her heart, at her gut. That maybe he'd been relieved to walk away from her, from their rocky marriage.

"When I saw the announcement," he added, "I rushed here as fast as I could."

"Turns out you could have finished your coffee," she said, then walked over to the window and stared out. A huge Christmas tree decorated the town green in the yard, colored lights and tinsel wrapped around it.

She turned back to him, half expecting him to be gone, this all just a dream. He was so damned good-looking. And wearing clothes she'd never seen before, clothes the Theo Stark she'd known would never have chosen. Cowboy boots, for one. Theo had liked expensive and very comfortable Italian black leather boots for winter. And these worn, faded jeans that looked so incredibly sexy on his long, muscular frame? Theo liked dark clothing—black pants, black button-down shirt. The black leather jacket was more him, though this one had a rugged look she wouldn't think he'd have gone for. The sunglasses he'd been wearing, though—pure Theo.

Where have you been all this time? she wanted to ask. *Why didn't you get in touch, somehow, someway?*

But she couldn't form words. She could only stare at him, drink him in, as questions crowded her head.

She suddenly realized he was frowning now and it snapped her back to attention.

"Allie," he said. "What did your fiancé mean about the baby? 'One baby, sure.' What was that about?"

"Well, at least I was right about that part," she said. "You really don't know."

His gaze narrowed on her. "Know what?"

That we're both getting the surprise of a lifetime today, Theo. You're not only alive—but the father of baby quadruplets!

She reached inside the top of her jacket and pulled out the gold locket her sisters had given her, flicked it open and held it out to him.

He stepped closer and squinted at the little picture.

He looked back up at her. "Four babies. Quadruplets? Who are they?"

She clicked shut the locket and dropped it back under the jacket. "They're your children, Theo."

Allie watched Theo take a step back, shock on his handsome face. As she thought, he really and truly hadn't known. Allie was surprised someone *hadn't* kept tabs on her for him. Then again, she had no idea how these things worked—law enforcement officials faking their deaths for protective reasons. But Allie was well acquainted with every nuance of Theo Stark's face and features. He'd had no idea he was a father.

Maybe—very likely—Theo had told his contact *not* to update him on Allie and her life. She'd bet anything that was the case.

"What?" he said, staring at her, his eyes full of disbelief. *"What?"*

She nodded. "I found out I was pregnant a couple days before you—" What? Not died. Walked away. For almost two years.

"Oh, Allie," he said, shaking his head. He stepped toward her, and she could tell he wanted to pull her into his arms, but this time it was she who took a step back. "I'm a father?" he added in a tone she'd never heard before. A mixture of fear and wonderment.

"The night you were— The night of the explosion," she said, "I'd planned to tell you I was pregnant."

She'd never forget how she'd felt when the pink plus sign had appeared in the tiny window on the pregnancy test. That maybe a baby would save their five-year marriage. Then the sinking heart when she knew full well a baby shouldn't and couldn't save a marriage. They'd have to do that on their own and they'd failed miserably for the past year. So she'd kept the news to herself as long as she could, until she'd been bursting with it. But Theo hadn't come home at all that night she'd been determined to tell him, to sit him down and demand they work out a plan to save their marriage. Because of the baby. In spite of the baby.

There were four babies. And then no marriage to save.

"You were pregnant," he whispered, his voice breaking.

"With quadruplets," she said. "Boy, did you dodge a bullet. Literally." Ha ha, she thought miserably and then burst into tears, her hands flying up to cover her face.

He pulled her into his arms and she let him, her stiff muscles releasing against him.

For months after his "death," she'd wished she could feel his arms around her. Despite how worried she'd always been about him, Theo had always made her feel so safe. Even at the end, when their marriage was falling apart, he'd hold her and she'd believe all over again. They'd be okay. They'd work it out.

"Why didn't you call me? Text me? Something, anything?" she said. "How could you have let me think you were dead when you weren't? How?" Tears streamed down her face. If she had raccoon tracks, it was fine with her. She'd earned them. She pulled away from him and grabbed tissues from the box on the table.

The look on his face pierced right through her. "I couldn't risk it, Allie. I can't tell you how many times I held a prepaid cell in my hands, burning with need to hear your voice, to tell you. But I couldn't."

She took a breath and dabbed under her eyes with the tissue.

"We have a lot to catch up on," he said. "*I* have a hell of a lot to make up for. But walking away from you was the hardest—the worst—thing I've ever had to do."

"But you did it," she whispered.

He walked over to her and took both her hands in his. "A serial killer made a direct threat against you. All I cared about was keeping you safe. With me—the one witness who could put him away—gone, he had no reason to go after you."

She gasped. But then shook her head. She wanted to know everything and didn't want to know anything. Or maybe just not now.

He closed his eyes for a moment and then walked toward the window, glancing out. "And, yeah, knowing how miserable I was making you, how I was failing as a husband, I thought the split-second decision I made to fake my death was the right one."

There it was. He'd said it, the actual words. He'd faked his death. Fake, fake, fake.

"It was, at the time," he added. "I'll tell you all the gory details if you want to hear them, when you want to hear them. Including the call I got from the FBI agent and US marshal that McBruin was killed early this morning. But right now, I just want to be with you. And I want to see my children."

The little faces of her quads floated into her mind. A calm came over her and she found she could breathe normally again. "Two look just like you. One looks like me. And one looks like the both of us. People always comment on it."

His eyes lit up. "Boys? Girls?"

"Three boys and a girl," she told him.

"I'm a father," he whispered. She caught his shoulders slumping in defeat. If there was ever a move that wasn't Theo Stark, that was it. Defeat wasn't his thing.

In fact, their rocky marriage, his admission of failing in that department, had to be a big part of what had allowed him to walk away and leave her behind. "All this time, I had four babies." He shook his head, letting his face fall into his hands.

"They're amazing," she said. "Healthy, happy, wonderful little humans."

His expression brightened and he managed something of a smile.

"Theo, where've you been all this time?" she asked.

"A cattle ranch in a remote part of Wyoming."

She raised an eyebrow. "You were a cowboy?" Suddenly the clothing made sense.

He nodded. "I learned fast and worked hard. I can't tell you the number of cowboys on that spread who were runaways from their lives in some form or another."

"That's sad, Theo."

"I know. But I'll tell you something. Hard, honest work makes a person think. Three quarters of those guys cleaned up their acts."

"I'm glad to hear it. I guess you're among them. You came home the minute you heard the serial killer was dead and that it was safe." She looked out the window beyond him, then back at Theo. Her husband. "So I suppose you'll get your job back."

"I plan to, if they'll have me after everything. If things go my way, though, I won't start back at the PD until after New Year's. I'd like to focus on us, Allie. On our family. I have four babies I haven't met."

She stared at him. "I didn't expect you to say that. I figured you were just telling me you're alive and then be off chasing the bad guys."

He shook his head. "My priority right now is you. Us."

Tears stung her eyes. "Before that night, you told me that maybe splitting up was what was best."

"Maybe it was then. I feel like a different person now, Allie. I can't explain it. I just know I died for you. Literally and figuratively. That told me how I felt about you, not that I needed to be told. I knew. I also knew I was a terrible husband and everything you never wanted. I was breaking your heart every day."

"I remember," she said. "So now what?"

"Now, if you'll allow it, I'd like to come home. Start over."

"It's not going to be like it used to be," she said. "My life is about a very serious schedule of taking care of four eleven-month-olds. And I work hard, too, Theo. My personal chef business really took off after— People hire me for all kinds of cooking gigs. If I'm not in the nursery, I'm in the kitchen."

"And now I'll be there to help out," he said.

So he was just going to move back in? Step right back into their lives? That sounded crazy.

"Theo, we didn't work before. You didn't want to start a family. And now there are babies in the mix. Four babies. What makes you think you're going to want this life now?"

"I just know I have a second chance, Allie. And I want to take it. I know I said I never wanted kids. But now that I *have* kids, that knocks that right out of the water."

A second chance. Her own thoughts right before he'd knocked on the door came back to her: *because she'd give anything for her old imperfect life back, a second chance.*

"Staying out of obligation started to destroy our marriage," she reminded him.

"I'm a father now. I take that responsibility seriously. I have eleven months to make up for, Allie. Not to mention the fact that you went through the pregnancy alone. Under terrible circumstances."

He'd barely been able to handle having to be responsible to a wife waiting at home, worried sick about him as he volunteered for the most dangerous task forces to rid Wedlock Creek and surrounding towns of crime. Adding four babies to that? He wouldn't last a week.

Maybe they both needed to see that, know that for sure, and then they could go back to their separate lives. Or maybe he'd surprise both of them. She was rooting for the latter.

She still loved Theo Stark with every bit of her heart. But she didn't want their old marriage back or him to be unhappy out of obligation to her—and now to his children. So they'd give it a shot. See if he could really become a family man.

"I guess I'll just go let the officiant know he can cross me off the list," she said. "Then we'll go home."

He put the sunglasses and Stetson back on. "Home," he said, closing his eyes for a moment. "You have no idea how happy that word makes me."

Chapter Three

As Theo pulled the pickup into the driveway of Allie's house—their house—he could see one of her sisters (he was pretty sure it was Lila) hanging a gold banner across the front door.

Congratulations, Newlyweds!

Oh, Lord.

"They're here!" he heard Lila shout toward the house as she rushed back inside.

He stared up at the narrow old white Victorian, his heart skipping a beat. Over the past two years, he'd dreamed of this house, the small, cramped two-bedroom fixer-upper that had been perfect for him and Allie as young newlyweds. They'd grown out of it fast, but Allie had always been so nostalgic about the place and they'd begun to talk about adding on a room. Of course, Allie would start talking about it as a nursery and Theo would shut down, thinking of it as more a spare room that would simply give them more space, more breathing room. A man cave for him and a library for all her cookbooks and recipe files. They'd never gotten around to the addition.

A tree near the front door was festooned with a few wraps of white lights. Allie loved Christmas; he was surprised she hadn't decked out the place with the usual holiday fervor. A few lights, a wreath on the front door. That was it.

"Oh, God, my sisters," Allie said, her gaze on the gleaming, glittery banner. "I'd better prepare them," she added, opening the truck door. "Wait here a sec, okay?"

He nodded and she got out of the truck and faced the porch.

Lila and Merry, two of the three MacDougal triplets, came rushing out of the house and started throwing what looked like rice up in the air.

"Congratulations to the bride and groom!" the sisters shouted in unison as rice dropped down all over Allie.

Who just stood there, shaking her head. Her sisters were peering at her, frowning.

"Allie? What's wrong?" Merry asked.

"I—" Allie began. "It—" she stuttered. "The—" Her shoulders slumped and she turned toward him with an *I need help here* expression.

Oh, hell, Theo thought, as he got out of the truck and took off his sunglasses.

Allie's sisters stared at him, then at each other, then at Allie, then back at him.

"Theo?" Merry whispered, squinting at him.

"What?" Lila said, mouth hanging open.

"I have only good news," Allie said to her sisters. "Theo, it turns out, is alive. And Elliot got cold feet. The timing couldn't have been better all around, actually. I easily could have had two husbands right now."

Merry crossed her arms over her chest. "We left you to get married and you come home with your dead husband. Explain yourself *now*."

"Right now," Lila seconded.

Allie brushed rice out of her hair. "There came a knock on the door that changed everything," she said, glancing at him. "And there Theo was. Very much alive."

Theo knew how much Allie loved her sisters—they were very close. But he also knew Allie and could tell she was exhausted and needed to sit down—lie down—and process everything.

"It's a long story," Allie said, "but has to do with the serial killer he'd been after. He had to fake his death to protect me. The psycho is dead now, so Theo was able to come home."

Her sisters narrowed their eyes at Theo.

He nodded. "I can explain further. Later, I mean," he added. "Once Allie and I have had a chance to talk."

"Thanks for watching the babies," Allie said to her sisters. "I'll take it from here." She gave her sisters the look, the one that meant *please just go and don't ask questions; I'll tell you everything later*. They knew that look.

Thanks for watching the babies. His children. His four children. Four precious little beings he'd never met, held, seen. His heart lurched and he turned to brace a hand on the hood of the pickup.

"I'll get our purses," Merry said, rushing inside and coming back out a moment later. "The babies are fast asleep at the moment, Allie. They've only been down for about ten minutes, so they should nap a good hour and a half."

Allie thanked them, and the pair left, walking toward town, which was just a few blocks away. Last he knew, the sisters were roommates, sharing a condo right in the middle of Main Street. He could only imagine the conversation they were having right now.

Allie gave him something of a smile-nod and started up the three steps to the porch. The last time Theo had walked into this house, there'd been only the two of them. And he counted as only a half, since he had put only half of himself into his marriage, their home life, those last few months. The rest he'd given to his job.

As he walked in the front door, the familiarity of the place almost did him in. He'd missed this house more than he knew. He'd built a life here with Allie and everything in it was a reminder of who they were at various ages. Twenty-four. Twenty-seven. Twenty-nine.

He walked through the foyer and into the living room. It was exactly the same. Big overstuffed couches. The muted area rug. The white brick fireplace. A big bowl of apples was on the kitchen island, as always; Allie loved apples. Upstairs, the master bedroom, not much bigger than the other one, hadn't changed, either. The gray-and-white paisley comforter. Allie's perfume bottles in front of the big round mirror of her dressing table. And on the bedside table—his side—the police procedural novel he'd been reading was still there, right next to the lamp and alarm clock.

The book was still there.

Which told him that, fiancé or not, Allie hadn't moved on. Not really.

His relief almost buckled his knees.

He turned around, and there she was, right behind him, biting her lip. He glanced down at her left hand. She wasn't wearing her wedding rings—the ones he'd put on her finger. Instead, a different gold ring was on her ring finger.

Maybe she *had* moved on. Maybe she just hadn't gotten around to putting the book on the bookshelf in the living room. Hell, maybe she was reading it. Maybe she slept on that side now. Nearer the door. For convenience.

"The babies are in the spare bedroom?" he asked.

"It's not the spare room anymore," she said with something of a smile. "It's the nursery."

He nodded. "The nursery."

Across the hallway he stepped toward the closed door. He put his hand on the doorknob and gently twisted it, pushing the door open and peering in. Low music was playing: a lullaby, he was pretty sure. The room was dark, black-out shades on the two windows. Four white cribs, each with a chalkboard with the baby's name in colored chalk hanging across the outer bars, were against the walls. He stepped across the big round blue rug of yellow stars and stood in front of one of the cribs. He closed his eyes for a second and then opened them. *Olivia*, read the chalkboard. A baby, his *daughter*, lay sleeping on her back in purple footie pajamas, one hand thrown up by her head in almost a fist. Her lips quirked.

"She's beautiful," he whispered.

"That's Olivia," Allie said. "On the left is Ethan."

He moved to the crib on the left and looked in. Ethan lay on his stomach, facing away, but then he turned his head and was now facing Theo. He had Theo's dark hair, as Olivia did.

"And across the room are Tyler and Henry," she said.

He moved to Tyler's crib. He also had dark hair, but there was something in his little face that was all Allie. Henry had the same dark hair, but it was harder to tell whom he looked more like, especially with his eyes closed.

"Four babies," he said, looking at the cribs, at the tidy room. "How have you done this on your own?"

"Well, this afternoon is a good example of how. I didn't give them lunch. Geraldine—you remember her from next door?—babysat and fed them lunch while Merry and Lila were at the town hall with me for a bit, then my sisters relieved her and put them down for their nap. Easy-peasy when you have a lot of help."

"You can't have help every minute of every day, though," he said.

"No. And there have been hard moments, hard hours, hard *days*. But no matter what—the lack of time, privacy, inability to pee in peace, drink a cup of coffee while it's hot, lack of sleep, staying up for hours with a sick baby only to have two or three sick at the same time, the screeching in the supermarket… I could go on. No matter what, I *have* them. They're the reward, you know?"

He did know. "I always felt that way about you, Allie. No matter how hard things got those last few months here. You were still my wife. We were still the Starks."

She almost gasped, and he wasn't sure if she was

touched or shocked or what. Part of him felt as though he knew her inside out. But he'd lost two years. And now he felt he didn't know her at all. She'd "buried" her husband. She'd raised quadruplet babies on her own for a year. She was obviously strong in ways he hadn't been here to witness.

Was she still his wife? Could they pick up where they'd left off—even if things between them had been rocky? Or given how troubled their marriage had been then and all the time that had passed—not to mention the big lie of his death—was it just too late for them?

He sure hoped not.

"I wish I could hold them," he said. "I want to pick them all up and tell them their dad is here, that I'm home." He stared down at Tyler, running a light hand along his back, covered in his green pajamas with tiny cartoon dinosaurs. This was his baby. His child.

"Oliva, Ethan, Henry, Tyler," he said. "I don't think they're named after anyone in our families. Did you just like the names?"

"They're named for you," she said. "In the order they were born."

"Named after me?" he repeated.

"The first initial," she said.

Tyler, Henry, Ethan, Olivia. *T. H. E. O.* He stared at her, so touched he could barely breathe, let alone speak.

"I had so many names and nothing sounded right or felt right. My parents. Your parents. Our grandparents. Aunts, uncles. I'd settle on a name, but it just wouldn't stick for some reason. And then I thought, there are four letters in Theo and four of them. And that was that."

He reached for her hand, and she let him hold hers for a moment. “I won’t let you down again, Allie. Or them.”

She stared at him but didn’t say anything. Finally, she said, “I could use a cup of coffee. You?”

He nodded and followed her out of the nursery and back downstairs. In the kitchen, she brewed coffee and he was about to get out the mugs when he realized he couldn’t just go poking around in her cabinets. For almost two years, this had been her house. Not his. Not theirs. Hers.

“You tell me, Allie, how you want this to go. I mean, are you comfortable with me moving back in? Do you want some time?”

She got out the mugs. And the cream and sugar. “This is your house, too.”

“It hasn’t been for a long time, though. I want to be here. I want our second chance.”

She turned and looked at him. “Me, too.”

Their relationship would have to be different because everything had changed; they were parents. That realization settled something in his gut, gave him hope. They had something—four very special somethings—concrete to spur them on to make their marriage work.

“So I live here again?” he asked.

She smiled and nodded and poured the coffee. “It’s going to be awkward for a few days, I’m sure. We have a lot to catch up on. Things between us weren’t good two years ago, though.”

“I know. My fault.”

She shook her head. “There were two people in this marriage with expectations. Not just one.” She sat at the kitchen table and wrapped her hands around the mug. Theo sat across from her.

"Are you disappointed about Elliot Talley?" he asked, taking a sip of his coffee.

"Disappointed at not being Allie Talley?" she asked and laughed.

He loved the sound of her laughter, rich and full.

"Allie Talley," he said, unable to hide his smile. "Talk about dodging a bullet," he added, hoping she'd find that funny and not inappropriate or offensive.

She smiled. "Right? Seriously, I'm glad he got cold feet. If I'd had to end things between him and me, I would have felt terrible. He's a good person and I'm happy for him that he realized he was in over his head."

In over his head—because of the quadruplets, he realized.

"What about me?" he asked. "How do you think I'll do?"

"Well, you're a different animal altogether, Sergeant Stark. You serve and protect—it's your motto. Whether you want this particular life is the question."

He tilted his head. "You mean the life of a family man."

He hadn't wanted it before—yet. Was he ready now? He didn't know. But the babies were here and that was all that mattered.

She nodded.

"I have responsibilities," he said. "I'm not about to shirk that."

"Waaah! Waah! Waaaah! Waaah!"

"Well, here's your chance to find out how you'll do,"

Allie said, standing up. "The quads are awake. I'll take two, you take two."

He felt a little sorry for the two who would get stuck with him. He'd probably put the diaper on backward. Then there'd be the awkward hold as he tried to figure out exactly how to balance the baby against him. General stiffness. He'd held babies here and there and had some basic skills training in delivering a baby, so he wouldn't be completely useless upstairs. But when he tried to remember the last time he'd picked up a baby, he couldn't. Allie's sisters didn't have children, he had no siblings, so there were no little nieces and nephews being thrust into his arms. Nor had there been any on the cattle ranch.

He followed Allie up the stairs and into the nursery. He watched her pick up Tyler and then lay him on the changing table, making quick work of changing his diaper. He went over to Ethan's crib and reached in, his heart hammering so loud in his chest, in his ears.

He picked up the little guy under his arms, Ethan's hazel eyes big and curious as he stared at this stranger bringing him to his chest.

"Hey there, little dude," Theo said. "You could probably use a diaper change, and I'm your guy."

Ethan grabbed his ear and laughed.

"I know. Ears are funny," Theo said, unable to stop staring at the baby's face, at how much he looked like a combination of him and Allie. Allie's eyes, his nose. His mouth, Allie's expression. The hair color was his; the texture, thick and wavy, was Allie's.

"I've already changed three babies and you haven't

even brought poor Ethan to the changing table," Allie said on a laugh.

"Oh, right," he said, rushing the baby—his son—to the changing pad on the second dresser. He knew how to change a diaper, of course. Basic baby care had been part of his police academy training, as were lots of necessary useful life skills he'd need on the job. But changing this diaper was different. This was his baby.

"I'm just teasing," Allie said. "I've had lots of practice. You've had none." His face must have fallen, because Allie bit her lip. "I didn't mean it like—"

"It's okay," he said. "You're absolutely right. I haven't had any practice. But I plan to change a lot of diapers."

She laughed. "Fine with me."

He turned his attention back to the baby on the pad in front of him. Taking off the diaper was the easy part, as was chucking it in the lidded diaper pail beside the changing table. Ethan kicked up his chubby little legs, making squealing sounds. Theo smiled at him.

"Watch out that he doesn't pee on you," Allie said. "Diapers are right inside the top drawer with cornstarch and ointments if he's chafed."

Theo's eyes widened and he grabbed a diaper and the container of cornstarch. He gave the creases of the baby's legs and his bottom a good sprinkle. Then he slid the diaper under Ethan. It took him a few seconds longer than it should have to figure out where the sticky tabs were folded, but he got the job done. He wriggled Ethan's legs back into the pajamas, then held him against his chest, relishing the scent of him—baby shampoo, cornstarch, *baby*.

I'm your father, he said silently to Ethan, staring at him. *You're my son.*

"You take Olivia," Allie said, gesturing at the freshly changed baby girl banging a teething ring against the bars of the crib as she sat and made *ba, ba, la* noises. "One in each arm. The family room is small, but it's babyproofed and they can crawl and pull up to their hearts' content."

The family room. No such room existed two years ago.

He scooped up his daughter, mesmerized by her thick dark hair and her green eyes—so like his—and her dimple, which was all Allie's.

"Ba da!" Olivia squealed as Theo cradled her against his left side, Ethan on the other.

"Hey there, little lady," Theo said. *I'm your father*, he added to himself. He'd introduce himself to them all downstairs.

He followed Allie to the family room, which used to be a dining room they'd rarely used unless they had company. Now the room was painted a lemon yellow with two murals of zoo animals on the walls. Foam mats with letters and numbers covered the floor and everything in the room had rubber edges. There were Exersaucers, a big playpen, tons of toys and stuffed animals, and a bookcase adhered to the wall, full of little books.

Allie set her two on the mat and so did Theo.

The babies began crawling, and he watched them with wonder. He lost track of who was who, his heart sinking.

"I guess it's easy for you to tell the three boys apart,"

he said. "I forget who was wearing what. Well, I know Ethan is in the green pajamas, now that I think about it."

"They're color-coded. Ethan is always in green. Tyler is always in blue. And Henry is always in orange. Lucky Olivia gets whatever color I feel like. I can tell the boys apart, but it's easier on my sisters and Geraldine or whoever else is helping out if we have a system we can all rely on. This way, no one misses a meal or gets fed twice or doesn't get a turn at this or that. That kind of thing."

He looked from Ethan to Tyler to Henry, taking in the colors and studying their faces, their hair, their expressions. "Ah, Tyler has more intense features than Henry. And Ethan has lighter hair than his brothers. Ethan and Tyler have hazel eyes. Henry's are green like Olivia's."

She nodded. "There are lots more differences. They may be quadruplets, but they're very individual. Olivia loves mashed chickpeas, but her brothers will fling them at the wall if I dare put the smashed beans on their trays. Ethan loves chocolate ice cream, but Henry will only eat vanilla. Tyler is the most adventurous eater. Loves all vegetables, too."

Theo smiled. "I have a lot to learn about them." He looked at the four, crawling and playing and pulling up and babbling. "As you said, they're all so beautiful and healthy and happy. I never want to leave this room."

Allie laughed. "Oh, give it a good twenty minutes."

He reached for her hand but felt her hesitation. He had to give her time. He knew that. He couldn't just waltz right back in.

Maybe we should take a break, he remembered saying just a week before his "death." He'd come home late, after two in the morning, and Allie had been awake and frantic. He'd been so laser-focused on the McBruin case he'd forgotten to call or text, and he'd completely forgotten they were supposed to go to her good friend's thirtieth-birthday party on a dinner cruise. She'd been looking forward to that, had bought a new dress. And he'd forgotten it all. They'd had one whopper of an argument that night, everything under the sun had been brought up and flung. She wanted to start a family. He wanted space. She wanted more of him. He wanted to be able to do his job as needed.

Maybe we should take a break...

He'd been shocked he'd said it, not sure if he meant it or not. The hurt in her eyes, the way her face had crumpled had rattled him, floored him, and he hated how he still hadn't known in that moment if they should take a break or not. He always felt like he had the answers, knew how to handle himself and the world. Except when it came to Allie and their marriage. He'd been floundering, sinking, breaking her heart every day, every night.

Let that go and start with now, he reminded himself. *You're not the same person you were two years ago. Neither is Allie.*

He sat down on the floor and let the babies crawl over him, scooping up one and then another and blowing raspberries on their pj-covered bellies. He'd always thought that when people said that their children's laughter was the best sound in the world it was a cliché, but now he got it. There was no more beautiful sound. Particularly baby giggles.

"Da-da!" Henry said, throwing a foam block at him and laughing.

Theo sucked in a breath. “Did he just call me da-da?”

“Well, to be honest, they call all men ‘da-da’—the mailman, the teenaged checkout bagger at the supermarket, George Futters three doors down, and he’s ninety-two. It’s developmental at this age.”

“Except this time, Henry got it right,” he said, unable to shake what had to be a goofy smile on his face. He picked up Henry and held him out a bit, running a finger down his impossibly soft cheek. “You’re right, Henry. I am da-da. I’m your daddy.”

Allie burst into tears.

“Hey,” he said gently, Henry in one arm while he reached the other out to her. “What’s wrong?”

She wiped under her eyes. “I just never thought I’d hear that. That *they’d* hear that. Their father saying ‘I’m your daddy.’ Holding them. Being here.” Tears rolled down her cheeks, but she was smiling at the same time.

He nodded, unable to speak, his chest feeling way too tight to contain his heart.

He picked up Tyler. “I’m your daddy,” he said, kissing the top of his head. Then he did the same with Ethan and Olivia.

“Well, I guess the introductions have been made,” Allie said, grabbing a tissue from the box on a shelf and dabbing at her eyes. “I have to say, Theo, this is going well.”

For once, he’d made her cry in a *good* way.

But he still heard the *so far* that she hadn’t added.

But then it was Olivia’s turn to throw a foam block at Henry, which started a round of shrieking, and he watched Allie turn into supermom, gently disciplining Olivia with a “no throwing,” and suddenly Theo was right in the thick of it all, feeling very much like he belonged.

It was only when he'd glance at Allie that he'd feel a distance, a disconnection. Babies were easy. No history. They didn't talk. You took care of them and loved them and nurtured them and all was well. Allie—his wife—was a whole other story.

But he'd been waiting almost two years for this moment. And he was going to make it work—no matter how hard it was or how long it took.

Chapter Four

A few hours later, Allie was in the kitchen, dropping fresh ravioli into a pot of boiling water. She had some frozen ravioli and tons of easy-to-defrost-and-reheat dishes in the freezer, but tonight felt special and Allie wanted to cook. The quads loved her four-cheese ravioli in a simple butter glaze, and Theo had always loved it, too, but with her grandmother's amazing garlicky marinara sauce and garlic bread.

She could hear Theo in the family room, talking to the babies. He was finding his way in interacting with them, talking to them, and it made her smile. *Ah, Tyler, I see you like screeching at the top of your lungs when one of your siblings dares go after the toy you were aiming for. You could get a job as a screamer in a horror film with that set of lungs.* Then: *Why yes, Olivia, it's fine for you to bang that stuffed rattle on my knee. Thank you.*

A bit earlier he'd tried reading them a story but had quickly discovered eleven-month-olds didn't sit quietly for story time. He'd given up on that and crawled around the floor with them, and her heart was about to burst, so she'd excused herself to the kitchen to start dinner.

As if this were the most normal thing, her husband, her children's father, playing with them in the family room while she cooked. As she gave the ravioli a stir, she pinched herself to make sure this wasn't all a dream. It wasn't.

Her phone buzzed with a text. Her sister Lila.

Well??? We're dying for info here!

She smiled and texted back: All good. He's playing with them.

We're still in shock.

Her, too. Join the club.

See you sometime tomorrow for the deets. Xo

She was draining the pasta when she realized she was still wearing the Irish friendship ring that Elliot had given her when he'd proposed. She put the big pot back on the stove and then took off the ring and put it in the mishmash drawer of menus and rubber bands.

She looked at her left hand. *That's better*, she thought, wondering about her wedding rings. Her rings and Theo's were in her jewelry box upstairs, in the bottom drawer that she never opened. Should she put them back on? Give him back his?

Or should they put them on when they felt more settled?

She had no idea, but dinner was ready, so she tried to put the rings out of her head and headed into the family room. Theo was on his hands and knees, playfully calling out, "I'm gonna get you," the babies crawling and giggling.

This was all I ever wanted, she thought, watching them. *And now I have it. This has to work*, she told herself. *We will make this work.*

Even if he felt like a stranger right now. He wouldn't always, right? He'd been back in her life for just a couple of hours. She had to give it time.

We will earn back those rings.

"Dinner will be ready in a few minutes," she said. "You grab two, I'll grab two?" she suggested.

She said it like she said it every day. She could seriously get used to this. Live like this.

"I'm on it," he said. "Okay, you two," he said to the babies closest to him. "Time for dinner! Here I come!" They squealed and he scooped one up in each arm, Olivia beaming at him, Ethan grabbing his ear and giggling.

Whose house is this? Whose life is this? Where am I? Afraid she'd burst into ridiculous happy tears, she quickly reached for Henry and Tyler and followed Theo, marching and making *fi, fi, fo, fum* noises, into the kitchen.

"We certainly weren't figuring in quadruplets when

we bought this place," he said, trying to maneuver Olivia's legs into the high chair seat. Not easy with another baby in his other arm. He finally got her settled, then slid Ethan into his seat, giving the harness a click.

With the babies in their high chairs around the kitchen table, cut-up ravioli on their little plates, Allie watched Theo discover the joys of trying to eat dinner with four eleven-month-olds sitting between them.

You do want kids, though, right? she'd asked him on their third date when she knew, without a doubt, that she wanted to marry him, that he was the one. He'd been talking about his plans for the future, about making detective, then sergeant, then, hopefully one day, captain.

Someday, he'd said. *Right now I honestly can't imagine.*

At twenty-four, that had sounded right to her. She hadn't been necessarily ready to be a mother at twenty-four, either. And so she'd married the love of her life, the man of her dreams, counting on someday.

Except he couldn't imagine having children at twenty-nine, either, when their arguments had begun to turn from his dedication to his job to his refusal to give her a timeline for starting a family. The last year of their marriage was a doozy. If he couldn't agree for them to get pregnant when they were turning thirty, then when? *Then never*, she'd known.

During their engagement, when she'd told him she wanted to marry in the Wedlock Creek Chapel, but, nudge-nudge-wink-wink, there was that legend about the multiples, so they might have quintuplets next year, he'd said: *Does anyone really believe there's a fertility spell on the chapel? Come on.*

Allie believed. Wedlock Creek was chock-full of multiples, of all ages, produced by people who'd gotten married at the century-old chapel. Of course, she knew plenty of couples who'd married at the chapel who had singles or trouble getting pregnant at all. Still, she liked to believe and so she did.

But Theo hadn't been ready for kids, so Allie dutifully used birth control. And then that crazy night when it had failed her—failed them… She and Theo had been arguing, neither refusing to budge from their points, their "rightness," and then Theo had shaken his head and said he was sorry and just pulled her into his arms, and they'd both shut up. He just held her and she'd gripped him, wishing things could be different, as she knew he did. And when he kissed her, she kissed him back and he'd made love to her on the couch with tenderness and passion and she felt his love like she hadn't in months.

She'd conceived the quadruplets that night.

But the next night, he'd forgotten they'd had plans to attend an award ceremony—her sister Merry was receiving a Brewster County Elementary Teacher of the Year Award—and he'd been unreachable, something she hated. He'd come home at 3:00 a.m., full of apologies and a reason she couldn't fault him for, involving a cop down and a manhunt. And on and on it went, the hurt and stewing, the two leading different lives, their connection breaking up. Those last few weeks, when he'd reach for her, she'd turn away.

"Nothing like a piece of buttery ravioli hitting you on the cheek," Theo said now.

Allie startled; she'd been so wrapped up in the memories she'd disappeared there for a moment, something she hadn't had the luxury of doing the past eleven months.

"I meant to tell you to watch for flying ravioli bites," she said a moment too late, as a little piece of cheese pasta landed on her shirt to the accompaniment of baby laughter.

"No, no, no, Henry Stark," Allie said firmly. "No throwing food."

The baby boy picked up another piece of ravioli and put it in his mouth.

"Excellent job this time, Henry," Theo said, quickly eating a few bites himself. "Never a dull moment, that's for sure."

She took a sip of the white wine she'd poured for them. "Oh, the dull moments are plenty, too. Trust me."

He laughed and took a sip of his own wine. Theo loved a particular kind of local craft beer, but she hadn't bought that in forever. She'd certainly pick up a six-pack tomorrow. And some of his other favorites. He liked those salty pretzel rods. And coffee-chip ice cream. Everything bagels and vegetable cream cheese. English muffins with sharp cheddar cheese. Tomato juice, which she also loved. She had plenty of that. "The ravioli is delicious. As always. I've missed your incredible talent in the kitchen."

"You were always fun to cook for. You love everything."

It was one of the few areas they'd never had issues. She cooked, he ate with gusto and appreciation. No matter what recipes she tested on him.

There were a few more flung ravioli pieces, but the babies were fed and then it was bath time. There Theo was on his knees beside her in front of the tub, four little ones in the bubble bath. With his help lathering up wispy hair and gently washing backs and necks, the four Stark kids were clean and in fresh pajamas lickety-split. There was more playtime in the family room, and then it was time for bed. The quads were each settled in their cribs, the lullaby player on low, the black-out shades down and just a soft lamp illuminating the glider chair.

"I usually read them a story before bed," she said, sitting down and reaching toward the bookshelf beside the chair.

"I'll do the honors."

She smiled and got up, sitting down on the heart-dotted beanbag chair her sister Merry had bought as a Valentine's present.

Theo went to the bookshelf and pulled out a few books before making his choice. She was surprised he differentiated. He sat down in the glider, the lamp illuminating his face, his gorgeous face that she'd dreamed about almost every night.

"This book is called *Four Little Ponies*," Theo said, glancing through the bars of each crib, then back at the book in his hands. "'Four ponies live in a big yellow barn,'" he began and read the story about the pony brothers and sisters.

By the time he finished, Allie was half asleep herself, his voice lulling her. It had been one hell of a day and she was exhausted.

The book finished, he got up and peered in all the cribs. She saw that the quads were asleep—well, except for Henry, whose little eyes were drooping, drooping... Ah, now he was asleep, too.

"Well done," she whispered.

He smiled. "I think a piece of ravioli landed inside my shirt. I could use a shower."

A shower. Suddenly, the thought of Theo Stark, six feet two, one hundred ninety pounds of gorgeous maleness, naked in her shower, sent a delicious, long-denied frisson of heat through all her nerve endings.

"I'll just grab my bag from the truck and be right back," he said.

"One bag? That's all you have?"

He nodded. "I was a ghost the past two years. Ghosts don't require much."

Her heart squeezed. She couldn't begin to imagine what his life had been like all that time. She wanted to know everything. About the cattle ranch. What his assumed name had been. If he'd been in constant contact with the FBI agent and marshal. How that had all worked.

But Theo was already heading down the steps and out the front door, so she'd save her questions for when he returned.

And boy, did she have a lot of questions.

Theo put on his sunglasses and Stetson before he stepped out. The sun had long set, but the houses were close together in this neighborhood and he didn't want to freak out any of the neighbors with his presence just yet. Freaking people out was on the agenda for tomorrow morning.

The cold mid-December air was bracing and refreshing. Theo grabbed his duffel bag from the back of the pickup and slung it over his shoulder, again struck by the lack of Christmas at 22 Wood Road. The neighbors' houses were all lit up; two doors down there was even a Santa and his reindeer in a sleigh lit up on the roof.

But Allie, who loved Christmas, had barely strung lights around one tree. As if she'd have time, he realized. Village rallying or not, Allie had been alone the past two years. She'd gone through what must have been a difficult pregnancy without him. Raised the babies for a year without him. She'd clearly given everything to the quads and taken little for herself.

He came back in the house to find Allie sitting on the second step, her blond hair in a ponytail. She popped up. "Master bathroom is still in the same place. Everything you'll need is there."

He nodded. "Thank you." He headed up the stairs and into the bathroom, which was surprisingly roomy for a small house. He stripped naked and turned on the shower, then stepped in under the hot spray. Man, that felt good. His big frame had been stuck behind the wheel of the pickup for several hours this morning; then seeing Allie and explaining himself had stiffened his muscles even more. Now he could relax. He soaped up and washed his hair, using Allie's shampoo, a clean, fresh smell he'd always associate with her.

Five minutes later, dressed in faded old jeans and a long-sleeved T-shirt, he emerged from the bathroom, slicking back his hair. Allie was coming out of her bedroom—their bedroom?—and stopped dead in her tracks.

"I didn't hear you come out," she said, staring at him. "Water pressure okay? Hot enough?"

She was nervous, he realized. "Shower was great. Did the trick. I feel like a million bucks."

"Good," she said. "Because I have questions."

He nodded. "I'm sure. And you deserve answers. I'll tell you everything, Allie."

She eyed his clothes. "All your things are in the attic. I couldn't bear giving your stuff away, but my sisters convinced me to at least move your clothes out of the closet."

He thought of her opening their closet every day, seeing his clothes… He couldn't imagine how painful that must have been. "I can understand that. I'll get everything later."

She nodded, and once again, he followed her down the stairs, this time to the living room.

They sat down on the sofa, each at opposite ends, slightly facing each other.

She pointed to the silver urn on the fireplace mantel. "So what's really in there?"

He grimaced—at her question and at the sight of the urn. Shame gripped him at what he'd put her through. "I'm not sure."

For a moment she looked furious and he didn't blame her. "I want to know the whole story," she said. "What happened that night?"

He took a sip of the wine she'd moved to the coffee table. "You know I was on a joint task force—a few cops from the PD and the local FBI field office—to catch serial killer Leo McBruin."

He saw her shudder at the name. Everyone had heard of McBruin for months before that fateful night. A serial killer in Brewster County. There hadn't been a murder in Wedlock Creek in seventy-five years. Suddenly, a murderer was lurking very close by. Theo had been obsessed with catching the guy, putting him away.

"You okay?" he asked. "I know this is a lot to take in, a lot to hear."

She took a sip of wine and let out a breath. "No, I want to hear it."

He nodded. "You know I witnessed him kill a man a couple weeks before that night, but he got away. A lead I followed led me to cross paths with McBruin in an abandoned warehouse on the outskirts of Wedlock Creek. It was almost midnight and my shift had long ended, but I had to check it out. So I went alone, figuring I'd call for backup if it panned out. And there *he* was. Fifteen feet away."

He heard her suck in a breath this time and he moved closer to her, unsure if he should continue.

"I want to hear it," she said. "I'm okay, Theo."

"We locked eyes. He said, 'You.' And I knew he recognized me as the witness. He had the coldest eyes I'd ever looked into."

"I'll bet," she said, shaking her head.

He nodded. "I'd gone from a cop who was hunting him to a witness who could testify against him. It was just the two of us in that building. I stayed hidden to assess my shot. But ten minutes into this, he'd clearly done some research on his phone. He started rattling off names of law enforcement officials on the task force, including me. Then he started addressing me by name. And letting me know that he was going to enjoy killing my pretty wife. Her two sisters, too."

Allie gasped. "My sisters?" What? Lila and Merry had been threatened, too?

He nodded, closing his eyes for a moment. "And then McBruin said, 'And your dad, who can't remember his own name in the old folks' home. Room 241. Cozy setup he has there, Stark.'"

"Oh, Theo," she said, her voice choked.

He tried to keep a lid on the old rage, the panic that swamped him whenever he thought of those moments. "McBruin was taunting me, trying to get me to come out so he could get a shot at me. Finally, I saw him move into the doorway, then throw something in—a bomb. He ran out, laughing."

"But you made it out," she whispered, her face turning white.

He nodded. "McBruin didn't know that. The explosion destroyed the warehouse, but I'd been able to take a running slide through a shattered part of the back wall and slither through into the dense woods behind it. I was scraped up pretty bad, but no broken bones."

"Your captain and two officers came to the house in the middle of the night," she said, her eyes flat. "They told me you were dead. That your barely identifiable body was found in the debris. They said they had your wedding ring, engraved with *Forever, Allie* inside. Your badge, your ID. How'd you set all that up?"

He hung his head, then looked her in the eyes. "Once I was hidden well enough in the woods and heard a car fire up and peel out, I knew McBruin was gone. I called my FBI contact and reported what happened. I told him he had to announce my death immediately to protect you and your sisters and my dad. It was a split-second decision, but the fed agreed. With me 'dead,' McBruin would have no reason to go after you or anyone close to me as leverage."

The thought of anything happening to Allie, to her family, because of him… It was too much for him to even think about now.

"The plan was for me to disappear and provide further intel as needed on a burner phone, and he would let me know the moment McBruin was either caught or dead. That day finally came very early this morning."

"Whose body was found in that warehouse?" she asked, gripping her wineglass.

"No one's," he said, the shame spiraling again. "There was no body. The FBI agent made it up, got it squared away with a US marshal. He'd met up with me that night and I gave him the ring and my ID, then he handed me some cash so that I could disappear. And I did."

"Oh, God," she said, putting down the glass and wrapping her arms around herself.

"And with how bad things were at home, how I was destroying our marriage, breaking your heart on a daily basis, I thought at least you could start over, find someone who'd make you happy."

"But you *did* come home," she said. "What if I'd found that person? What if I was happy and settled?"

He stared at her, unsure what she was saying. Was she disappointed he'd come back? It might not have worked out with Talley, but maybe she was hoping for another nice guy with a safe, more predictable job as a husband and father for the quadruplets.

Regardless, he had to tell her the truth.

"I hadn't planned on coming back," he finally admitted. "The plan was to stay dead, no matter what, to let you have the life you deserved."

"Then why did you come back?" she whispered, her voice breaking.

"The minute I hung up with the agent and marshal this morning, all I wanted was to come home, Allie. To see you. To tell you I was alive. To beg your forgiveness and ask for a second chance. I didn't expect to feel all that, to need to be with you the way I did. But I wanted to come home more than anything."

She reached out her hand and touched his arm. "I'm very glad you didn't stick to the original plan, Theo." She swiped under her eyes and he wanted to move even closer to her, to hold her in his arms and tell her, *Me, too*, but she'd lifted her chin and seemed to be thinking and assessing and he didn't want to make emotional decisions for her. He stayed where he was.

"So you didn't love what's-his-name?" he asked.

"Not like—" She stopped and leaned her head back. "I was marrying him for the kids. To set up a secure life for them. I needed a life partner and he seemed a good safe bet."

"I can understand that." The thought had bile churning in his gut, but he did understand. Another man almost stepped into his life, would be raising his children, loving his wife. Living the life he'd almost thrown away. His gaze went to her ring finger and he realized that other ring she'd had on was now gone. *Good.*

"And the FBI agent and the marshal didn't mention your wife had quadruplets while you were away?" she asked.

"I doubt either knew. They kept watch on you for a solid month after my 'death,' and when it was clear that you, your sisters and my father weren't in danger, that everyone truly believed I was dead, that was that. I guess you weren't showing at that point or hadn't told anyone you were pregnant."

"I did keep it under wraps until I popped," she said. "My sisters knew, but I didn't tell anyone else until I was four months along."

"I admit I didn't ask for information about you because I didn't want to know, couldn't handle knowing." He'd thought about her day and night as he'd made his way south to the middle of nowhere on that cattle ranch he'd heard was looking for hands. But knowing anything about her life would have leveled him. "We should toast to Elliot Talley," he said. "For getting cold feet. Or you'd be a bigamist and we'd have a problem on our hands."

She gave a rueful smile. "Right?" She scrubbed at her face. "I'm so tired. Have I ever been this tired? Even right after the quads were born?"

"It's been one hell of a day," he said. "Why don't you go up to bed? I can sack out here."

What he'd give to lie beside Allie. The thought of it, of his wife next to him in bed, had gotten him through many nights in the bunkhouse on that ranch.

She shook her head. "You're my husband. I'm your wife. If we're going to make a go of this, let's not put more distance between us. There's no need for separate bedrooms."

Hope shot through him. "I feel the same way."

She glanced at him. "I'm not talking about sex," she

added. “That I’m not ready for. Not until we rebuild some intimacy. We were sorely lacking in that department two years ago.”

He nodded. “Understood.” He wanted her, desperately. But even the thought of touching her, feeling her, making love to her, made his knees weak. He needed to get some control of himself anyway. They could both use the space—together.

She stood up and so did he. Tonight, for the first time in almost two years, he would lie beside his wife, the fantasy that had kept him going all those lonely, awful months becoming reality.

Chapter Five

Allie lay very still, barely able to breathe. Beside her, in the space that had been empty for the past two years, was Theo Stark. He wore a T-shirt and a pair of blue sweats. She was in her usual bedtime attire of T-shirt and yoga pants. She had a dresser drawer full of sexy lingerie that hopefully one day she'd open again.

They were both on their backs, staring up at the ceiling.

Awk-ward.

She turned on her side, facing him, propped up on her elbow, which prompted him to do the same.

"I'm glad you came back," she said. "I just wanted to make sure I actually said that, that it didn't get forgotten in everything else that needed to be said."

He smiled and seemed to be looking at every bit of

her face, taking her in, studying her. It was so strange how you could feel someone's love and be so unsure at the same time.

She wanted to reach out and touch the hair against his neck. He'd let it grow out shaggy and it was so sexy she was having trouble keeping her hands to herself. Usually his hair was regulation-short out of habit, first the military, then the police department. And he'd always been muscular, but two years of ranch work had his arms ripped like she'd never seen.

"I can't tell you how good this bed feels," he said, his green eyes on hers. "My bed at the bunkhouse was basically a cot on springs. The pits."

"Did you have friends, at least? The men you worked with?"

"I kept to myself mostly, but bonds were built at the ranch. You're there for one another even if you don't know someone's last name or where they came from. A lot of the guys liked to talk about their pasts, what drove them away. I kept my mouth shut, of course."

"And..." She bit her lip, unable to ask. She didn't want to know.

"And what?" he asked, holding her gaze.

"Women," she finally said.

"Only you in my fantasies, Allie, and I'll swear on that."

Tears stung her eyes. That was becoming a bad habit.

"Hey," he said, stroking her hair. "Everything's a lot to take in. It'll get better."

She managed to nod. If she spoke, she'd squeak. "I want you to know that Elliot and I, we never, I mean, we..."

"I was *dead*, Allie. You had my ashes in an urn on the mantel. Whatever happened while I was gone is understandable."

"We kissed, but that was it. He never even saw me naked."

"Wait. You and Elliot Talley never had sex?"

"Nope. It just wasn't like that."

He turned onto his back and stared up at the ceiling and she felt his hand suddenly on hers, turning it over and holding it. He looked at her and she squeezed back.

"This is some conversation," he said.

She laughed. "Right? Can we change the subject?"

"Please," he said.

"So how was the food on the ranch? Did you eat chili every night?"

"Pretty much. Lots of grilled burgers and corn on the cob with the freshest butter you ever tasted. One of the barn guys made it. No one ever used his real name, they just called him Butter."

She smiled. "You love corn on the cob," she said.

"It helped, having it so often and being so far from everything I knew and loved. Especially because you're such an amazing cook. I missed your crazy meals."

She laughed. As a personal chef, Allie often needed to try out recipes in advance and she'd use her husband as her tester. He loved everything, unfortunately, so he really wasn't a good guinea pig. "So tomorrow you'll go see your captain?" she asked.

"Yes, but things will be different, Allie. I don't need to join task forces that will put me in the position I was two years ago. I'm a father of four. I'm needed here just as much as I am on the street."

"You'll be happy as a regular ole cop?" she asked.

"I'll be happy because of you and the quads."

That really didn't answer the question, though. And it was what she was most afraid of. The novelty of having a family might wear off and he'd long to get back out there, be the law enforcement officer he wanted, needed to be. And then they could be right back where they started.

"The US marshal said he'd call the captain on my behalf to explain in an official capacity. So I'll go see the captain, then my dad."

Allie pictured Clinton Stark sitting in his favorite overstuffed chair in the Alzheimer's wing of the nursing home, a wonderful center where he'd been for five years, four in the secure wing.

"I visit your dad every week," Allie said.

She felt Theo freeze beside her. "Really?" he asked.

She nodded. When they were first dating, Theo used to talk a lot about his father, how frustrated he was by him. The two men had had a difficult relationship all their lives, despite how similar they were. Theo's dad was hardheaded, very stubborn, and they had very different worldviews. That had always been tough on Theo, who'd idolized him as a kid and wanted to be a cop like his father and follow in his footsteps. Their relationship had started to fall apart when Theo was a teenager and disagreed with his father on just about everything but the most basic tenets of law enforcement.

Then early-onset Alzheimer's had begun taking his father's memory to the point that he hadn't recognized Theo. She knew Theo hated that he felt he'd lost a huge part of his father before they could make any kind of peace. Before the night that had ripped apart their lives two years ago, Theo had visited his dad a few times a month, sometimes staying five minutes, sometimes staying hours. He did what he could handle.

"That was kind of you," Theo said. "He couldn't know who you were, though."

"No, but I know who he is. He's a connection to you. And our children's only living grandparent. I brought the quads a few times."

He turned onto his back again and she knew he was overcome with emotion and let him have some privacy. They were silent for a good minute.

"I appreciate that you kept up the visits," he said. "My dad always liked you. He thought I had life all wrong, except when it came to you."

She smiled. "I'm glad you'll get to see him tomorrow. They've decked the halls for Christmas. It's very festive there these days."

"Good," he said, nodding. He was quiet again for a minute, then said, "Speaking of Christmas, I want to make this one really special for the quads."

She could actually feel her heart puff out in her chest. "Me, too. It's their first."

"Well, you're the expert on them. I'll defer to you on presents."

"They got their dad back for Christmas," she said. "I'd say that's the best gift they ever could get."

He reached out a hand to her face and she held it there. She felt their fledging connection in every cell of her body.

There was hope here.

* * *

During the night, Theo heard a cry and bolted up. One of the animals?

Wait. The soft down comforter and fresh-smelling pillow clued him back in to where he was. As did the warm body beside him, the wavy blond hair splayed on the pillow.

He was home.

On the ranch, he'd shared a bunkhouse with four other guys; each had his own very small efficiency-type apartment in an outbuilding very close to the stables and barns so that they'd wake from any sound of distress. But the sound he heard—that he just heard again—was a baby crying. His baby.

Allie stirred and turned over, fast asleep. He glanced at the clock on the bedside table. Five twenty-two. Well, no wonder he hadn't woken up naturally. Alarms went off at five thirty on the ranch. And no wonder he felt so well rested; he'd had a full night's sleep and on an amazingly comfortable mattress.

He carefully got out of bed so as not to disturb her. His muscles were a bit stiff, given that he'd tried so hard to keep from accidentally touching Allie during the night. He'd wanted to curl up around her and wrap his arms around her, and once or twice he'd rationalized that she'd want that, too, but he'd said he'd take it slowly, not rush, and he owed her time to get used to all this. To him. Being alive, being back.

He headed into the nursery and surveyed the cribs for the crier. Ah. Olivia stood in her crib, her face crumpled and red. At the sight of him, she held up her arms.

"Well, what's going on with you, my girl?" he

whispered, reaching in and picking her up. He held her against him for a moment, then set her down on the changing table and made quick work of a diaper change. "Better?" he asked. "Or maybe this is your regular wake-up time." Babies tended to wake up pretty early, he knew.

Her expression was happier even if her big green eyes were droopy with sleep. "Da ba," she said.

"Hmm, so maybe you're still tired and need another half hour," he said, picking her back up. He cuddled her against his chest as he sat down on the glider, rocking gently back and forth.

"Oh, give me a home, where the buffalo roam, and the sky is not cloudy all day," he sang softly, and though he was off-key and couldn't hold a tune, she fell asleep in record time.

He sat there and stared at her, in complete wonder at the sweet weight of her, her wispy silky hair, her adorable fingers. "I missed eleven months of your life. Your brothers' lives. I won't miss another minute," he promised.

He'd meant what he said to Allie earlier. When he spoke to the captain in the morning, if he'd be allowed back, he wouldn't let the job be his life. These *babies* had to be his life.

You said when we got married that I'd come first and I don't. I never do, Allie had said quite a few times over the years when he'd disappointed her time and again, putting his work over their anniversary, her birthday, weekend plans she'd made.

He had said that, made that promise to her. And he'd broken it. Not meaning to, not wanting to, but needing to. The drive in him to catch the worst of the worst, his specialty, had been implanted in him as a kid, as he'd witnessed his father, his hero despite their difficulties getting along, clean up the streets of the worst of humanity. Organized crime was well hidden in even the small, idyllic towns in their county, but his dad had made it his mission to keep the people of Wedlock Creek safe, to the point that he'd risked his life over and over, taking a bullet that put him on desk duty until he'd retired, kicking and screaming—figuratively—that it wasn't fair. Theo's mom had died when he was young, so his dad and an aunt were all he'd had. Now it was just his dad and he didn't even know Theo, wouldn't recognize him when he visited later.

Didn't matter. Theo had been ridding Wedlock Creek of bad guys in his dad's name for a long time. But now he hadn't just made a promise to Allie; he'd promised his children. They had to come first. And they would.

"I promise you, sweet pea," he said to Olivia, dropping a kiss on her head before putting her back in the crib.

Not bad, if I do say so myself, he thought. *I'm getting the hang of this and it's still my first day as a father.*

But a second later, he heard Olivia fuss, then cry. He hurried back over to her crib just as Henry let out the wail of all wails. Then Tyler joined the party. Only Ethan lay silent in his crib—to the point that Theo rushed over to him to check that he was breathing.

He was. Theo's heart rate slowed. "Okay, three screaming babies. What do I do?"

"WAAAAAH!" screeched Ethan.

Make that four.

He figured Olivia was set, since he'd just changed her. She probably just wanted to be picked up.

"Waah!"

"Waah!"

The waahing was coming fast and furious. Which crib did he go to? Whom did he pick up first?

He was frozen in the middle of the rug, wanting to put his hands over his ears like a three-year-old.

"They're mighty loud for such little creatures," Allie said, rushing into the room and picking up Henry. She stopped at Tyler's crib; he was standing up and squawking. She gave his side a little tickle. "Be right with you, sir." Then she did the same to Ethan.

"I've already changed Olivia," Theo said. "And then they all started crying at once and it's like my feet turned to lead."

Allie smiled when she probably wanted to throw a diaper at him. "It's chaos at first. But you'll get used to it. Why don't you grab Tyler," she said, putting freshly changed Henry back in his crib, "and I'll take Ethan?"

Theo set Tyler down on the changing table. "I think Ethan pierced my eardrum," he said on a laugh. A hollow laugh. He felt anything but lighthearted at the moment. He couldn't even handle the morning routine. Allie had done this on her own for almost a year.

"Did I mention the quads wake up between five and five thirty every morning?" she asked with a rueful smile. "It's hard for grown-ups to be night owls around here."

He *was* a night owl. That would have to change.

He held Tyler, feeling like a total flop as a father. Five minutes earlier he'd been New Dad of the Year.

"It takes time to work your own rhythm," Allie said. She'd always been good at reading his mind. Reading his body language. "There's four of them and only one of you."

He nodded. "I hear you. And thank you."

He had to get good at this. He could not let her down again.

Chapter Six

With the babies settled in their high chairs and eating every bit of their scrambled eggs and side of fruit without throwing any of it, Theo felt better about taking on fatherhood.

"What time are you calling the captain?" Allie asked over the din of Ethan banging his little fork, which he didn't exactly have the hang of using for eating, on the tray table.

"At eight. He's an early riser." He couldn't wait to hear his captain's—former captain's—voice and finally connect. He had no idea what the man thought about what had gone down. But Theo had a feeling Morgan White would say he would have done the same thing. Theo knew his captain would have.

She nodded. "Tell you what. Why don't I run up and

take a shower while you handle playtime in the family room, then we'll switch and you'll make your call?"

"Sounds good," he said. They each took two babies and settled them in the family room on the foam mats.

"Man, it's nice to be able to take a shower when I want," she said, glee in her hazel eyes. "See you guys in a few," she added and disappeared through the door.

He missed her immediately. In record time she was back, her shoulder-length hair damp and waving sexily down to her shoulders. She wore jeans and a pale pink sweater.

"Your turn," she said, her smile lighting her entire face.

"You don't have to rush anymore," he reminded her. "Take a twenty-minute shower tomorrow morning."

"I just might take you up on that. Of course, then there'll be no hot water for you."

More nights like last night, so close to her and unable to touch her? A cold shower might be in order. He smiled and turned to the crawlers. "Back soon," he said. "Be good for your mother."

He took a quick shower, dressed in running gear and then sat down at the desk in the bedroom and called Captain Morgan White on his cell phone.

"White," came the familiar voice, and for a second Theo was overwhelmed with emotion. His captain.

"It's Theo Stark," he said. "Agent Fielding brief you?"

"He did," the captain said. "Two years of your life, Stark. That's dedication. I don't know if I could have done it. Oh, hell, of course I would have. And I'm proud of you."

Theo smiled, feeling his shoulders, his muscles relax. "McBruin threatened everyone close to me. I had no choice."

"I know. Thanks to your intel, Wyoming is free of that psycho. Listen, I talked to the mayor. We never did promote anyone into your position, so your job is open. Even if it weren't, I'd insist on adding one for you."

Yes. The sense of homecoming felt complete now. His work. His family. His town. "I appreciate that more than you know. Captain, I made a promise to Allie that I'd wait until New Year. I have quadruplets, did you know that?"

"The whole town knows that, Stark," he said. "Even I've babysat those rug rats."

Theo laughed. "How'd that go?" he asked.

"Like you'd think. Hey, I'm about to leave for my five miles. Meet me at the park. I'll tell you about the short ceremony we're having in your honor at 5:00 p.m. today. I've already sent out a press release, so make sure you're there."

He laughed. "I'll be there."

"Oh, you poor dear!" said a woman whom Allie vaguely recognized from around town. The woman was staring at Allie's left hand. "You still haven't put on your wedding ring again."

Allie and most of Wedlock Creek, at least those who'd been able to attend today's special award ceremony honoring Theo in the town hall on such short notice, stood packed in the ballroom.

Lila and Merry, on either side of her, shielded her from the busybody. "The rings are being cleaned,"

Merry practically snapped and stood in front of Allie to block further conversation. Luckily the room was very crowded.

"I've heard that at least twenty-five times since I walked in," Allie said. "Mind your own beeswax!" she whisper-yelled, making a megaphone out of her hands.

"I like Merry's response," Lila said. "Keeps the gossips from squawking."

Allie nodded. When Theo had called her earlier and let her know about the ceremony, news of which was posted on social media, she'd thought about wearing her rings. She'd gone up to her bedroom and slid open the bottom drawer of her jewelry box, taking out the beautiful diamond ring and gold band. Farther back lay Theo's. She'd plucked it out, turning it around so she could read the inscription, *Forever, Allie.* She would never, ever forget the moment Captain White had given her the small plastic bag containing his ring. She hadn't gotten out of bed for two days and only had because of morning sickness.

She could have just slipped the rings on and given Theo his. They were married, after all. And Theo was back and they were carrying on. But putting on the rings felt as monumental to her as she and Theo making love again—the intimacy had to be earned, not forced. She'd put the rings back in the jewelry box.

"Talk about timing!" Eva Newton, who worked at the library, said to Allie, pulling her into a hug even though Allie barely knew her. "I heard that if Theo had been a minute later, you would have been Allie Talley." Her mouth dropped open, her eyes lighting up. "Oh, goodness. Allie Talley. Did you know that rhymes?"

This time it was Lila who moved in front of Allie, and as more and more people packed into the room, Eva was carried ahead by the crowd. Thank goodness.

"Suddenly Allie Talley doesn't make me laugh," Allie whispered.

"To be honest, it was never funny," Lila said, nodding very seriously.

That was the truth.

"You darling quadruplets!" said a woman from Allie's neighborhood, stopping to kneel down in front of the stroller. "What lucky little sweethearts. They have their daddy now. It's a Christmas miracle!"

Allie smiled and nodded. She liked those comments, and there had been plenty since word had gotten out about Theo being alive. Her children, their children, had their father back, and yes, it *was* a Christmas miracle, well, in a way.

"His selflessness in the face of grave danger..." Captain White was saying at the podium, to cheers and claps from the crowd.

Her husband was most definitely a hero. She just wanted to make sure that the hero really wanted the life he was stepping into. She'd been on her own with the babies a year now, since their birth, and she *could* keep going. But if he entered their lives and made them all love him and then couldn't handle family life?

She'd be shattered—again.

Her babies would cry for their father's attention.

And the arguing would start all over again. They'd be exactly where they were two years ago, except this time, there were children involved. Babies.

He'd promised her. But he'd promised her before and

the job had taken hold. So what the hell was she going to do? Let herself fall back in love with Theo?

Ha. She'd never fallen out. But she *had* been on her own. She would have to keep her distance, emotionally speaking, until she knew how things were going to be.

And Christmas was in two weeks. The holiday made a good mental deadline. If he couldn't put his family first for Christmas, he'd never put them first.

Hell, she wasn't even asking for first anymore. Just equal billing. He wasn't the only cop on the Wedlock Creek PD. He wasn't the only dedicated, brave, experienced officer who could join task forces and work with federal law enforcement.

She'd see.

And today, she'd be proud of the man she'd married, who'd given up his life for her and her sisters and his father.

As Theo accepted his award to claps and whispers and exclamations of *Oh, my God*, Allie clapped loudest of all.

After the ceremony, Theo was mobbed by people—colleagues, neighbors, old acquaintances. All he wanted was to go home and be with Allie and the quads. He could see her, getting hugs from many, the giant four-seat stroller besieged by well-meaning people who were overwhelming the tykes. When all four started to cry at once, that was his cue that it was okay to excuse himself.

"Duty calls!" a colleague said to him with a smile.

Theo did a double take. Yes. His children were his duty just like his job had been. If he thought of it that way, it would make it easier on him to put them first.

"Ready to get out of here?" he whispered to Allie, who was being pulled into a hug from behind.

"Oh, thank God," she said.

He smiled. "Let's go."

They made their way out of the packed room, saying goodbye and thank-you and *Yes, it's a miracle, a Christmas miracle.*

Finally, they were outside and he quickly got the babies loaded up into their car seats in his pickup. Then he and Allie raced inside and he sped off.

"You okay?" he asked.

"More than okay. My husband is alive. My babies' father is back. I knew there would be comments and questions. I guess I'm just still a bit in shock. I like how the captain ended his speech. 'Welcome home, Sergeant Stark.'"

"I don't think I could ever put into words just how happy I am to be here."

His eyes on the road, he felt her gaze on him, assessing and wondering. He had a lot to prove to Allie. He knew that.

"So what's next?" she asked. "You're going to see your dad? We could go with you."

He glanced at her. "Actually, I'd appreciate that." It had always been hard on him to visit his dad, his only living relative who didn't know who the hell he was.

Suddenly, with his family by his side, he felt less unsettled.

Theo had called ahead to the Wedlock Creek Nursing Home to alert the director and his dad's aide that he wasn't dead after all, his job made easier by the fact that they'd heard all about it on the local TV news and read about it on social media. When they arrived at the home, his father's aide brought the family to the second-floor community room, where Clinton Stark was sitting in front of the big window on the second level, looking out.

A well of emotion rushed Theo and he took a step back. He hadn't seen his father in so long, and even if the man didn't recognize Theo, he wanted to tell his dad he was alive. Maybe it would get inside somehow and his dad would *know.* Two years ago, Allie had been the one to go to the nursing home and share the terrible news with Clinton. Theo sucked in a breath as he imagined that conversation, Allie likely in tears, trying to hold back the flood, his dad looking confused why this sweet, angelic lady he'd never seen before was crying on his shoulder and hugging him.

He owed Allie so much, he thought, realizing he was just standing there, lost in memories while Allie was waiting for him to go up to his dad. Clinton was facing away from them, and as Theo walked up beside him and knelt down, he realized his dad was looking out at the brightly decorated Christmas tree in front of the home.

"Hey, Dad, it's me, Theo," he said, taking his father's thin, veiny hand. "Have I got a story for you." As his dad turned toward him, a smile lit up the man's face. He noticed Allie take a few steps back to give them some privacy. He told his dad the basics, aware Clinton Stark wasn't following and wouldn't remember and didn't even know who he was. But it felt good to tell him face-to-face. His dad had been told he was dead. Sometimes he was grateful that his dad couldn't remember him.

Every now and then, before Theo had left two years ago, his dad would have these amazing moments of clarity, oftentimes just for a few seconds. He would know who Theo was, and for that precious little while, Theo forgot about their old problems and just wanted to be in that place of connection with his father, a man he'd once idolized.

"Dad," Clinton said with a smile. "It's good to see you." He reached for Theo's hand.

Theo choked up, his eyes stinging. He blinked back hard. Theo knew he looked a lot like his late grandfather.

He held his father's hand tight, glancing at Allie, who had tears misting her eyes.

"No one's too old for time with their dad. Mom here?" Clinton asked, looking around.

"Just me today," Theo said.

"Good to see you," Clinton said. "Always so good to see you." The man yawned, his eyes drooping. In moments, he was asleep, his snores like a freight train, as always.

His aide, who'd been sitting nearby, popped up. "I'll take him back to his room for his nap. Glad to have you back, Sergeant Stark."

"Thank you," Theo said and watched the woman wheel his dad away. "Never gets easier," he said to Allie. "There's so much I want to tell him. And I can't."

"Well, you can," she said. "Even if he doesn't understand the way you want him to, it's you who needs to talk, you who needs to explain, you who needs to get stuff off your chest."

"We'll never make peace," Theo said. "That chance is long gone."

"You can make peace, Theo. With yourself."

He didn't see how. But a cry came from the stroller, pulling him out of his thoughts.

He knelt down beside the quads, one asleep, one almost asleep, one screechy—Olivia—and one shaking a rattle.

The noise was getting a bit much for this crowd, so they headed out.

When they hit the bracing cold December air, he suddenly had an urge to go running like he used to on the cattle ranch, or get in his pickup and take a long drive. To clear his head, to be alone. Maybe to push everything out of his head.

But Olivia was holding up her arms, and suddenly, making her happy and comfortable was more important to him than making himself happy and comfortable.

He'd call that progress.

And Allie, who'd always known him better than he liked to admit, was watching him take Olivia out of her stroller and cuddle her against him. The look on Allie's face was everything.

Chapter Seven

That night, with the quads asleep in the nursery—all at the same time, which had taken four trips in, two by Theo, two by Allie—Theo finally stretched out in bed. Today had been long and crazy, the award ceremony, the visit to his dad and a screech-fest on steroids from the quads after dinner taking more out of him than he'd realized. He was exhausted. But watching Allie put lotion on her legs had him wide-awake. The beachy scent of the lotion, combined with the long strokes of her hands on her legs, completely mesmerized him.

"I'm going to be honest," he said. "It's not easy being in bed with you and keeping my hands to myself. Especially when you do that."

"Rubbing lotion on my toes is sexy?" she asked.

"Yes, actually."

She laughed and set the lotion on the bedside table, then slipped under the covers on her side, facing him. But whatever she'd been about to say or do was interrupted by a loud cry coming from the nursery.

"Waah! Waah-waah!"

He waited another moment to see if the crier would soothe on her or his own—he'd learned that from the baby book he was reading—but there came another cry, and if the whole nursery got going...

Allie moved the blanket and started to get up.

"Stay and relax," he said. "You've been getting up all night for almost a year. My turn is long overdue. I've got it."

She smiled. "I'll admit, it's nice to hear someone say that.'"

He headed across the hall to find Tyler standing up in his crib, his face red and crumpled.

"What's the matter, little guy?" Theo asked, picking him up and holding him against his chest. He rubbed Tyler's back, but the crumpled face didn't uncrumple. He'd recently been changed, so maybe it was a matter of a tummy ache. Theo shifted the baby in his arms a bit and rubbed Tyler's little belly, and he began to settle down.

He sat in the glider and rocked Tyler until the baby's eyes were shut, but thoughts of his own father kept him in the chair, the feel of the little guy in his arms very soothing. His father hadn't been one to change diapers or help with homework or be there at all, actually. The job came first, and Theo had spent a lot of time alone and with his aunt Ellen, who didn't have a ton of patience for a loud, wild kid.

He needed to put his family first now. But what if that didn't come naturally? What if he didn't even realize he was neglecting Allie and the babies? He'd stay late at work to tie up ends on a case or chase a lead and suddenly it would be 2:00 a.m, and then what? That was what came naturally to him. But he didn't want to be the father his dad was. He wanted to be what the quads needed and deserved: present, there, in tune, aware. Allie had always said he'd be exactly the kind of father he wanted to be, but did it really work like that? He hadn't chosen to be a distant husband who'd put the job first; that was just in his DNA and what felt right.

Or was it? Could he choose? Or was he who he was?

He knew what they said about leopards. That they couldn't change their spots. But if you wanted something bad enough—this second chance—then you changed. It was that simple. And that complicated.

I have to do it for you, he whispered to Tyler, watching his little chest rise up and down.

By the time he went back into the bedroom, Allie was fast asleep, too, smelling like roses. He pulled the comforter up to her shoulders, and before he could stop himself, he kissed her cheek. Then he turned over and tried to sleep, but it was a long time in coming.

Over the next few days, life in Wedlock Creek and at 22 Wood Road settled down some—and so did Allie. People got used to the idea that Sergeant Theo Stark hadn't really died, after all. True to his word, Theo was a full-time family man. In the middle of the night, as Allie would stir and be just about to leap out of bed to see who was crying and why, she'd discover Theo already in the nursery, taking care of business. They'd gone grocery shopping yesterday, Theo taking half the list and two of the quads. And after dinner last night, he'd cleaned up—stacking the dishwasher, spritzing the counters and wiping them down, sweeping the floor. In bed last night, a new book was on the nightstand on his side: *Your Baby, Month by Month Till Two.* She'd smiled at all the Post-its.

He was trying and succeeding and Allie found herself letting her guard down a bit. Stopping to admire how handsome he was, how sexy. At night, they'd lie side by side, talking about the quads, about whatever funny or not funny things had happened that day, little things that needed to be taken care of around the house. Allie would find herself dying to touch Theo but holding back.

One touch, on his shoulder, would be all it would take. A kiss on his lips. And she could be back in her husband's arms. But it didn't feel right yet.

Because you're afraid, a little voice told her as she grabbed two cartons of eggs from the refrigerator. *Sex with Theo would pull you right back in, completely, mind, body, heart and soul, and then there'd be no piece of you left to protect.*

Focus on what you're making, she told herself, trying to put Theo out of her mind.

Today, while he was taking the quads out on his own to the baby play space on a playdate with one of his fellow officer's twins, Allie was catering lunch for the Gelman Girls Generation monthly get-together. Seventy-seven-year-old Virginia Gelman had started the monthly tradition so that she, her fifty-five-year-old daughter and twenty-seven-year-old granddaughter would spend time together every month, and she'd hired Allie on a standing gig to make something special for the third Saturday of every month. The hard part was that Grandma Gelman didn't eat dairy, her daughter didn't eat gluten and the granddaughter was a vegetarian.

So today, it was her spicy black bean burgers topped with avocado on a brioche bun—gluten-free, of course—with a side of sweet corn salad. While she added the sweet potatoes to the black beans, millet and spices in the big silver bowl, she focused on her work. Cooking jobs always calmed her. Her mind never wandered. She only thought of the people she was cooking for, what their needs and hopes were, and she wanted them to enjoy their food. If she put all of herself—and not a distracted mind—into the black bean burgers, they would be delicious.

An hour later, Allie had the burgers in a warming tray and the corn salad and dessert—her berry tart—ready to go. The Gelman Girls got together at Virginia's house each time, and though Virginia had welcomed her to cook there, she much preferred messing up her own kitchen than someone else's. This way, she could deliver, serve and then skedaddle, and worry about cleaning up her kitchen later.

Virginia lived in a Colonial just a few minutes' drive from Allie. When she arrived, her client welcomed her and sent her off to the kitchen to plate. The Gelman Girls, Virginia, Leanna and Maya, were in the living room, and not that Allie liked to eavesdrop, but she did hear some juicy stuff. Maya, the twenty-seven-year-old, was getting married in a couple of months, and her mother and grandmother were giving her advice.

"The key to a happy marriage is—" Virginia began.

Unfortunately, Allie had interrupted at the worst possible time by coming in to set plates of burgers and the bowl of corn salad on the dining table.

Nooo, she thought. *I want to know! Keep talking!*

"Allie could tell us all better than I could," Virginia said. "Imagine, your husband has to fake his own death to save your life and he sacrifices two years of his own on some dreadful cattle ranch in the middle of nowhere until the threat is gone."

"But wait," the twenty-seven-year-old said, heaping corn salad on her plate as she glanced up at Allie. "Weren't you about to marry someone else when your husband rushed home to stop the wedding?"

Allie felt her cheeks burn. "Well, I was thinking more of my quadruplets and their need for a dad. I thought theirs was—"

"Oh, you poor dear!" Leanna said, taking a bite of her burger. "Wow, is this good! Are you sure it's dairy-free?"

"Dairy-free, gluten-free and vegetarian," Allie said with a smile.

"She got her husband back," Maya said. "It's Elliot Talley who's the poor dear! Left at the altar!"

They all made commiserating noises as they ate. "I should let him handle my taxes," Leanna said. "After the holiday season, it's tax season."

Allie mentally rolled her eyes. And she *could* announce that Elliot had gotten cold feet and run screaming from the town hall before he even knew he was off the hook for proposing to marry a supposedly widowed mother of four lookalike babies, but that would make her feel petty and gossipy, so she just *thought* it.

"Anyhooooo," Virginia singsonged. "Back to what I was saying. The key to a good, long-lasting marriage is communication. You can't expect your husband to be a mind reader. You have to tell him what you want and what you expect."

The bride-to-be nodded around a bite of burger.

Her mother took a bite of corn salad and said, "Of course, I agree, but equally important is—" She paused for a very long sip of her white wine.

Get on with it, Allie thought as she made a show of giving the corn salad a stir. *I need to know! Equally important is...*

She really had nothing else to do and no reason to stay, so she headed for the kitchen to collect her things.

"Every day, every *single* day," Leanna Gelman Clark began.

Allie stopped in the kitchen doorway, her ears peeled.

"You do one thing that you know will make your husband happy," Leanna added. "Just one thing."

"Moooom!" Maya said, rolling her eyes.

"I'm not talking about sex," Leanna said. "Though that counts toward the one thing, of course." Allie saw the woman give her blond eyebrows a wiggle.

She had to hand it to this trio of generations of Gelman Girls. They could talk like this. Allie's mom had always blushed red-hot when the subject of sex had come up with her and her sisters. She smiled at the memory of her mom giving the triplets "the *big* talk," as she'd called it, the day after their group sweet sixteen at an ice cream shop. *Anything beyond kissing a boy will end up with you pregnant and heartbroken before you can even think about college, so say no, girls!*

Allie smiled. She wished her own mom and grandmother were here to give her advice and the wisdom that came from experience. Allie sure had experience but felt like she knew very little—particularly about marriage.

"Then what do you mean, Mom?" the bride-to-be asked.

Leanna took a fast bite of her burger and waited till she gobbled it down before responding. Allie loved how these women lived in dramatic pauses and made everything they said seem like breaking news. Allie, for one, was hanging on every word.

"One nice thing that you know will make him feel loved or happy or appreciated," Leanna explained. "In the morning, you leave enough coffee for him and set out his favorite mug. Or you buy chocolate eclairs because you passed the bakery and know he loves those things. Or while he's annoying you by yelling at the TV while watching a game, you give him a shoulder massage. Then instead of an argument with you telling him to keep it down, he's thanking you for the massage and you both feel appreciated."

"Huh," the bride said. "I get it. Just little things."

"But one thing, every single day," Leanna said. "And when you start doing that, guess what? He'll start doing the same. Then you're both working at making each other feel loved. Even twenty-nine years in."

"I wish I could send you two to Paris for your thirtieth anniversary," the bride said. "You might have to settle for somewhere very local and inexpensive if I'm treating."

"I'll treat," Virginia said. "And when you get to fifty-five years like me next year, an around-the-world cruise is in order—both your treats."

The Gelman Girls laughed and decided to actually eat instead of talk so much. Allie could listen to them all day.

She finally headed into the kitchen, ideas filling her head as she collected her stuff. *One nice thing.*

As she was walking to the front door, Virginia called out, "Allie, lunch was simply marvelous. You give that handsome sergeant a hug from us, will you?"

"I sure will," Allie said. She hadn't really hugged Theo at all since he'd been home, had she? She'd flung herself into his arms when he'd first appeared in the Bridal Preparation room, but that had been out of absolute shock.

Their second chance meant she'd have to step out of her comfort zone of keeping herself at a solid emotional distance. And a good start would be showing him that she did want their marriage to work, that she believed what he said, that he wanted to be there, that this wasn't about obligation—especially now that he had four children.

One nice thing a day. She drove back home making a plan.

As Theo arrived at Kidz Zone, a big, loud indoor play space a town over, he looked around for Reed Barelli. The Wedlock Creek detective not only had two-year-old triplets—two girls and a boy that came along with his sudden marriage to their mom, Norah—but twins who were close in age to the quadruplets. The Barellis, who'd been strangers an hour before their wedding, had married at the Wedlock Creek Wedding Chapel because of spiked punch at a town carnival. Now the former bachelor who'd been a city detective was the dad of *five kids under three.* And he looked really happy and together. *How* was the main reason Theo had asked Reed if he'd be interested in getting their crawlers together for a playdate, making it clear he needed and wanted tips.

And if Reed passed some intel on how he and Norah were not going nuts and making each other crazy, all the better. Theo had met Norah Ingalls Barelli at his award ceremony last week, and he'd seen them kiss at least three times—each with a baby in a carrier on their backs, and three in a stroller that rivaled the size of his own.

The man *knew.* And Theo wanted to.

After handshakes and introductions of the group—Reed's boys were Dylan and Daniel—they set the little ones loose in the "eight to fourteen months" play area with lots of pulling-up stations and things to press and squeeze. One of the greatest things about Kidz Zone, besides the gazillion age-limited play areas, were the smiley attendants who worked in zones, watching their charges like hawks. Parents couldn't take their eyes off their tots, of course, but the extra set of eyes right there was an extra bonus.

Theo had spoken to Reed on the phone for a good long time when they'd set up this playdate—about the McBruin case and how it had gone down. It had been so long since he'd been able to talk shop with an officer on the WCPD—and someone who instantly got it. Between that and having the multiples in common, Theo had made a very necessary friend.

"So tell me," Theo said, sipping the take-out coffee he'd stopped for earlier. "What's the number one secret to survival?"

Reed laughed. "I'll tell you—it's to aim higher than that."

"What do you mean?" Theo asked.

"Survival is base level. It's making it out of the house, period. Aiming higher is leaving the house without applesauce in your hair or a diaper stuck to the back of your leg. I don't know how that one happened, but it did. 'Detective Barelli, did you know there's a diaper on your thigh?' the barista at Java Joe's asked me once. Nope, hadn't known. Because I was operating on the baseline. That's survival instead of clockwork—it's clockwork you want to aim for, with some flexibility, of course."

"Clockwork—meaning according to schedule and without a hitch?" Theo asked.

"Exactly. Schedules, routine, organization—name of the game. Everything packed up and ready to go the night before, when the littles are asleep—make that when only *one or two* are crying bloody murder or throwing up all over your feet. Know what's what and be forearmed. Dylan here loves pears. Loves. As in he will stop shrieking in my ear, no matter the reason—if a pear slice lands in his hand. So guess what I always have in the baby bag?"

"I'm getting it," Theo said. "Be at the ready."

Reed nodded, then shouted out, "Daniel, don't bang the gong that hard." He turned to Theo for a second. "God, my *ears*." He took a swig of his bottled water.

"Then there's the wife. The key to success there is taking care of business."

"Elaborate," Theo said, sipping his coffee. "Please."

"Well, especially with multiples, your wife is going to need you to do what you say you'll do and to do stuff without even saying it or expecting a medal. That, my friend, is the key to smooth sailing in the Barelli household."

This was all gold, common-sense advice. "Huh. Take care of business. Don't expect a medal. Makes sense."

"Yesterday, I heard Rockwell on the phone with his wife—he's one of the rookies. And a rookie at women, obviously. I heard him say, 'Oh, I don't *do* anything? Who vacuumed the minivan last week? Who sprayed Febreze where Mikey threw up?'"

Reed laughed. "Yeah, keeping tabs and reminding of the one time you helped isn't going to win you any points. That I learned even before kids."

As baby Daniel was gleefully chucking balls at his brother in the ball pit, Reed stepped forward to clearly tell him no-go, but the attendant beat him to it. Meanwhile, Ethan was throwing balls at himself, which got half the babies in the pit doing that and giggling.

Reed laughed at the tots' antics. "How do you tell the boys apart? Are they color-coded?"

Theo nodded. "Ethan is green. Tyler is blue. And Henry is orange. Oliva gets any color. Apparently, she was purple until just last month when Allie said she just started looking more girlie in the face."

"My girls run around shouting their names for absolutely no reason these days, 'Bea! Bella!'" He laughed. "I can't tell you how happy Brody is not to be outnumbered. Of course, now with three boys, the girls are outnumbered. But it's one big happy family."

Speaking of which… Now for the most important question of all. "Tell me, Reed. How do you balance the job and family? What happens if you have to work late? Or you're chasing down a lead and don't want to stop?"

Reed took a sip of his water and seemed to be thinking about that one. "The balance happened kind of naturally, now that I think about it. I *want* to be home. I'm dying to see Norah and the kids at the end of the day. Yeah, sometimes it happens where I don't want to let a tip go and I text Norah that I'll be an hour or two late. But we've talked about that, and we're square on it. And I don't let it happen every day. Back when I was single, the job consumed me."

"It consumed me when I was married," Theo admitted. "But I know what you're saying. If I want to be home, I'll be home. That simple. Priorities."

Reed tipped his water bottle at Theo. "That, my friend, is the real meaning of life." He reached for his wallet and pulled a folded piece of paper. "I almost forgot—here's a free pass to my three-hour seminar on juggling multiples and the rest of your life."

Theo took the pass like it was the golden ticket. "Oh, man, do I need this."

For the next half hour, they watched their multiples crawl and climb and pull up and bang and squeeze and shriek to their hearts' content, and then it was time get home for naps. As he committed everything Reed had said to memory, Theo realized one thing he wouldn't have to work so hard at. He *was* dying to get home to Allie.

* * *

That night, as the Starks lay in bed, talking about how it had to be harder to have multiples of different ages than one set of the same age, Allie was struck with the urge to put her wedding rings back on. Not because it was "one nice thing" she could do for Theo, but because she fervently wanted the rings back on her finger.

Theo had surprised her over and over with how present he was, how involved in the quads' minutiae. He now could tell the boys apart just by looking at their profiles or how they crawled (Henry liked to stop and look around a lot whereas Ethan was Speedy Gonzales and Tyler preferred to just sit). And he was always suggesting this or that from the "Your Baby at 11 Months" chapter he was up to in the baby rearing book. Earlier he'd asked if they should get the quads used to sippy cups, since they'd be starting on cow's milk at the twelve-month mark. Questions she wouldn't expect to ever come out of his mouth, let alone be in his brain. The former Theo Stark wouldn't have had room in his head for all that stuff.

He is basically on vacation till January 2, she reminded herself. *Of course he has room and time and energy for you and the quads. He has no cases.*

That a slight chill ran up her spine clued her in to just how nervous she was about how things would be once the stack of case files did land on his desk. Old cases he'd inherit. New cases demanding immediate attention. Would he turn back into the Theo who broke her heart at least four times a day? Or would he be the husband she needed and wanted? The father their children needed?

Time would tell. But what she knew now was that she believed in him, believed in his vow and vows, believed that this second chance meant more to him than she even realized. And so she slipped out of bed and went to her jewelry box on the dresser.

She pulled open the bottom drawer and took out the rings. Her engagement ring, the gold band and Theo's ring. Her heart pinged at just the thought of putting these back on.

She turned to face him. "Will you do the honor of putting these back where they belong?"

He stared at her for a moment and she could tell he was emotionally overwhelmed. "Nothing could make me happier."

She got back in bed and gave him her rings, then held out her hand.

He took the wedding band and slid it on as he'd done seven years ago, then the diamond ring atop it.

"I hope you're going to put mine on my hand," he said, rubbing his ring finger. "I hated not wearing it. Every day on that cattle ranch when I'd look at my empty hand, it was like a symbol of losing you. The more I wanted that ring back on my hand, the more I knew I had to go home, that I had to try to change. Luckily, the quads helped push that along."

She smiled, warm flutters in her stomach. "They do come in handy that way, those needy little creatures."

He laughed. "Exactly." He held her gaze for a moment, his expression so full of tenderness that tears misted her eyes. Then he lifted his hand up to her and she slid the ring onto his finger. He took her hand in his and held on tight.

"I do love you, Theo."

"I love you, too, Allie. Always have. Always will."

Oh, foof. She wished he hadn't said that. *Always will.* It was like *Of course I love you, you're my wife. Of course I love you, you're my family. Of course I love you, we're related.*

Yes, he'd always loved her, and their marriage had fallen apart. So what did that mean for the future?

She looked at her rings, at the promise on her finger, and something struck her. What Leanna Gelman had been saying about marriage. It wasn't a one-way street. It wasn't up to Theo to do all the work. She had to, also. She had to help make this a marriage that could thrive and grow and be what they *both* needed, not just what she needed.

Theo loved foot massages. That would be a nice thing to do for him. Just because.

She moved to the end of the bed, sat on her knees, and at his raised eyebrows, she smiled, then got to work on his feet, which managed to be very sexy. She kneaded and pressed, and at his first happy groan of pleasure, she reached for the lotion he liked the smell of so much, and he sat back against the pillows on the headboard, watching her.

"I read in a magazine at the dentist's office a few months ago that feet are not an erogenous zone," she said. "How crazy is that?"

She froze for a moment. Why had she said that? She was bringing up what did or didn't sexually entice? She might be ready for wedding rings, but sex…

She wanted them to earn the intimacy, but truth be told—the intimacy would be too much for her. It would leave her unable to deny how in love she was. It would leave her vulnerable. Keeping that one gulf between them would keep her sane and safe.

She resumed massaging the deliciously scented lotion into his feet, working up to his ankles and shins. Such muscular calves, she thought, admiring his legs.

So much so that she didn't realize he'd sat up and was staring at her.

Oh, hell. She leaned her face forward. And so did he, slowly, as if giving her the chance to change her mind, back away, go back to just feet.

She wanted to kiss him so badly. She leaned forward more and kissed him, softly and then harder. He wrapped his arms around her and kissed her so passionately that her mind went blank for a second, wonderfully blank. All she felt was pleasure and sensation and him.

"There's more where that came from when you're ready," he said, pulling away a bit.

She looked at him with wonder. Huh. How had he known to stop things there? She hadn't even known that was what she wanted and needed until he pulled back. She wouldn't have been ready for more.

She'd done one nice thing for him and he'd done something nice for her.

Those Gelman Girls really knew their stuff.

"Oh, Allie," Theo said, lying back down. "I have a surprise for you. Well, I hope it's a good surprise."

"A surprise? What?" she asked, a burst of excitement blooming. Then again, between his surprising her with the fact that he was alive and her surprising him with the news that he was a father of four, maybe they could use a break from surprises.

"I can't tell you. Duh," he added with a smile. "I'll show you tomorrow morning."

Tomorrow couldn't come fast enough. She just wasn't sure she'd be able to sleep or not.

Chapter Eight

"How is my sweet Olivia supposed to sce the surprise if she doesn't put on her coat?" Theo asked the baby girl after spending ten minutes on the job. So far it was Theo 0, Olivia 10.

"Same goes for Henry," Allie said, trying to put the boy's little arms through the fleece jacket with the cute bear ears.

"And it's a surprisc for *you*, Olivia," Theo said, finally getting her coat on. "And your brothers and your mom. There! The Starks are ready to go."

"This Stark really wants to know what the surprise is," Allie said as Theo pushed the stroller out the door and down the ramp on the side of thc porch.

"It's about a ten-minute drive from here," he said, opening the back of the SUV for the stroller.

Ten minutes from here? Allie tried to think what was that distance away. Because they lived right in town, everything could be reached in seconds.

After they got the quads in their car seats and buckled themselves in, off they went, Theo turning onto main roads. Finally, he turned and drove down ranch lands, cattle and sheep grazing, horses in their pastures, enjoying the almost-fifty-degree weather in Wyoming in December. They passed a pretty yellow farmhouse and then Theo turned into a long driveway lined with evergreens.

She had no idea where they could be headed. A petting zoo at someone's ranch?

Finally, a gorgeous white farmhouse came into view with a red barn beside it, a black weathervane atop it. The house and barn looked straight out of HGTV Does Wyoming—pristine and yet rustic at the same time. She loved the barn-red door and black shutters, the twinkling white lights decorating the big bay window. The MacDougal triplets had grown up in a farmhouse like this one, not quite as pretty or grand, but they'd also had a swing hanging from two big trees.

Theo stopped the car at the end of the paved driveway. A huge wreath hung over the garage doors.

"What do you think of this house?" he asked her, unbuckling his seat belt. "It's a bit like the one you grew up in, don't you think?"

She nodded. "That was my first thought. Except this one is much prettier and fancier. It's like Chip and Joanna were here." At his *who?* expression, she added, "TV home show people."

"Ah," he said, looking at the house. "Five bedrooms,

three baths. Family room, finished basement. Deck off the back."

How on earth did he know all that? "Do you know who lives here?" she asked.

"I know who's selling it. An officer at the PD and his wife are moving to Utah to be closer to his wife's family. They need to sell fast. He was uploading the photos of it to get it ready to be sold and I thought, Allie would love this house."

She stared at him. "Wait, you mean you think we should buy it?"

"If you love it." He got out of the car and was around to her side before she could even touch the door handle. He opened her door and she stepped out, and then they got the quads into the stroller. "Let's go check it out."

He fished a key from the pocket of his leather jacket. "They're out buying moving boxes right now. They said we should take a look around. If we're interested, they'll sell to us. If not, they'll list it."

Allie stared up at the house. She couldn't even imagine living in such a big, grand home. She'd always dreamed of having a house like this someday. But *someday* had always been her old standby—not reality.

"And look—the Cohens already have a ramp for their strollers—they have three kids under six." He easily wheeled the stroller up the ramp, opened the door, and she followed him inside.

She gasped. It was as if HGTV had asked her for her dream requirements for a house, then brought her into one ready-made for her. The foyer opened into a huge airy space with vaulted ceilings, a loft above. To the right, a grand staircase curved high up. A wall of windows with sliding doors to the back showed a huge deck and a big backyard, fenced.

The kitchen was a chef's dream. The downstairs bathroom had a kiddie-size toilet and a regular-size one. There was a biggish family room with gorgeous light streaming through another entrance to the yard, and two smaller rooms, a den for each of them. Upstairs were five bedrooms, a huge master bedroom with the bathroom of her fantasies, including a spa-jet tub. The four other bedrooms were much smaller, but just right for kids.

"Our house was a starter house, Allie. Tiny and great when it was just the two of us, walkable to the PD and town. But we've outgrown it. And to be honest, the thought of what you had to endure there alone breaks my heart."

"What do you mean?"

"You grieved for me there. You were alone with four newborns there. You had to pack up my stuff and take it to the attic there. Maybe a fresh start in a house that fits us all is just what we need."

She thought so, too. She loved her house, loved that she had experienced all the good and all the bad there. That was life. But as she spun around, taking in the huge white-brick fireplace and the wall of windows in the living room, she felt renewed. A fresh start. For the six of them. "I'm not gonna lie. I love it. I already feel like I live here. That's how connected I feel to the house."

"I thought you would. When I saw the pictures at work, I just thought—this is Allie. And we'll barely have to do any accommodations for the quads because so much is already baby- and kid-proofed."

Her cup runneth over to the point that she couldn't speak for a moment. She looked around at the warm white walls and beautiful wood floors. She could see herself cooking in that kitchen, developing her business even more. She could see the quads taking their first steps in the big open space and running around the fenced-in yard. She could see them casting pennies in the wishing well and making wishes.

But were they moving too fast? He'd barely been back a week. They were supposed to be taking things slow.

This was a huge commitment. A new house.

"Theo, what if…"

"What if what?"

She bit her lip and looked outside, two shade trees making a perfect spot for a hammock.

"What if come New Year, you turn back into a pumpkin?" he said, wincing.

She whirled around. "Yes. Exactly. Well, not a pumpkin, but you get the drift. Right now you're a prince. You're everything I hoped for for the babies, Theo. But you're on vacation. What happens come March, April, when you're deep into casework? When the local FBI asks you to join a task force to go after organized crime spreading into Wedlock Creek?"

"Allie, I can't promise you that I won't give my all to my job. That's who I am. But I will promise you that I'll give my all to you and the babies, too."

And when you start resenting that you can't chase a lead or work till 3:00 a.m.…? That you can't risk your life the way you would have before because you have four children depending on you?

She really wasn't sure that he could make promises.

"I want this to work," he said. "And so do you. So we're committing. We're a family and this is a family house."

Committing. That was what she wanted, right? If she wanted it, she had to take the risk and trust him. "So we'll make an offer? Can we afford it?"

"We paid a premium for living right in town. That little two-bedroom will sell for more than this huge farmhouse will cost us."

"Wow," she said. "And all this space. No neighbors right on top of us. I can't even see any neighbors' houses!"

"Five acres," he said.

"Five acres," she repeated. "And a beautiful red barn with a weathervane."

"The house has plenty of room, but I was thinking the barn could be converted into a playhouse for the tykes."

Her babies, who'd had to share a nursery, would have their own *playhouse*. She shook her head with wonder, her cup seriously running over.

As Allie looked around, all she could think was that the house represented the future—their future.

"So we'll make an offer?" she asked, barely able to contain her glee.

He smiled. "We'll make an offer."

She threw her arms around him and he hugged her back.

"To new beginnings," she said.

"To new beginnings."

* * *

The next day, after he and Allie had slept on the idea of buying the farmhouse and decided to definitely make an offer, Theo was in the Wedlock Creek Police Department, shaking on the deal he'd made—thanks to Allie's real estate agent sister Lila—with Officer Cohen. Lila would put their house up for sale, and hopefully, things would move fast once all the usual stuff that had to be taken care of on both sides was done.

"Stark, got a minute?" the captain called over as Theo was heading out.

"Sure," he said, following the tall, husky man into his office.

The captain closed the door behind Theo, then gestured for him to sit down as he rounded the desk.

A closed door? What was this about?

"We've got a weird case and I'd like to handle it quickly and quietly, not start a hysteria," the captain said. "We have a Christmas-present thief on our hands."

Had he heard that correctly? "A Christmas-present thief?"

Captain White nodded. "Two houses, both in the same neighborhood, were hit up. One present from each home was stolen from under the tree. Both marked with a kid's name."

A simple burglary. Back when he was on the force, he hadn't had a case like that since his rookie days.

"Would you mind looking into it?" Captain White asked. "Detective Barelli has a huge caseload at the moment, and I'm not comfortable putting the rookies on this. Something tells me we're not dealing with a typical thief here."

"Breaking and entering?" Theo asked.

"Entering, but no breaking. Both times a side and a back door were left unlocked. Another reason I wanted to ask you was that the neighborhood is yours. Both houses are on Oak Hill Road." The captain handed over a very thin case file.

"I'll take care of it," Theo said. File in hand, he headed out, stopping at the desk in the far corner that would be his. The private area had been his "office" two years ago but had been turned into a makeshift meeting space. Now the captain had had it turned back into his office. He sat down in his chair, the familiarity making his heart skip a beat. This place, the PD, this office, made him feel as at home as that house had.

He read through the file.

42 Oak Hill Road. Owners reported a medium-size wrapped gift was missing from under the tree. They didn't think anything of it until they mentioned it, over coffee, to a neighbor four doors down, and she mentioned another neighbor had said a present was missing from under their tree. In both cases, no sign of forced entry; a side or back door had been left open. The parents questioned their children—in one home, a five- and seven-year-old, in the other a seven- and three-year-old—if one of them had swiped the gift, and the children insisted they didn't and a room check didn't turn up evidence.

That had been Theo's first thought, that a kid in the home had gotten antsy and wanted what was in that box marked for him or her. Tomorrow he'd pay the families a visit, get more of a sense of the situation.

As he was packing up, he overheard Reed Barelli

and another officer talking over a complicated case. There was suspicion of organized crime bleeding into Wedlock Creek, taking advantage of the increase in population that December always brought. The famed Wedlock Creek Chapel attracted Christmas and New Year's visitors who wanted to marry there for the holidays. A tip had come in about gun smuggling. The FBI had asked for the PD's help, and Reed and two other officers had been assigned. Come January, it was highly likely that Theo would be asked to join the team. Exactly the kind of case he liked. And exactly the kind that had destroyed his marriage.

Because he'd let it. The case wasn't sending Barelli off the deep end; he had five kids under three to get home to every night, and he did, leaving his work at the office, on the street. So would Theo.

But what if he couldn't? What if the call of the job was too strong and it became the priority in his heart and mind? What if he ended up thinking, *She'll just have to understand*?

And another thing. He wasn't even on the force yet, and now he had a case. Should he have turned it down, even though it was just a two-time present-napping? What if it turned into something bigger?

What if, what if, what if. *You decide. You choose. If you want your marriage to not just work but thrive, you'll make that happen.*

But the more he listened in on their strategy, the more he itched to rush over and offer some ideas of his own. Instead, he forced himself to think about mistletoe. He wanted to surprise Allie with a sprig for the doorway into the family room so she'd have to kiss him a lot. The old Theo would have assumed something green hanging from the doorway was mold and would have gotten rid of it.

So there was progress being made here. At least, Theo hoped so.

"Is that mistletoe?" Allie asked, peering up at the doorway between the hallway and the family room.

"Yes, yes it is," Theo said, a baby in each arm. "And since we're standing under it..."

"You have to kiss each baby," she finished for him with a sly smile.

He laughed and gave each beautiful baby a big kiss on the cheek. "And you."

Sneaky guy. She had to say she liked this side of Theo. Playful. Letting her know he wanted to kiss her.

She glanced up at the sprig of mistletoe and then puckered up for her kiss.

"Oh, that's sexy," he said, grinning.

"We each have two babies in our arms," she pointed out. "It's as sexy as we can get."

And were they supposed to be getting sexy?

He leaned forward and kissed her, and the moment his warm, familiar lips were on hers she wanted more, more, more. A deeper kiss. A longer kiss. She wanted him to pick her up and carry her upstairs to their bedroom.

But as she'd pointed out, they had four babies to get settled in the family room for playtime. An hour of crawling, pulling up, banging, babbling, making a ton of noise with gobs of toys gave the quads their fill of movement and they went happily into their Exersaucers, where they could scoot around and play with all the attachments.

With the babies engaged just a few feet away from them, Theo sat on the couch and patted the spot beside him. "Come sit. I want to talk to you about something."

She stared at him. Uh-oh. Those words were never about something good. When he wanted to tell her about the farmhouse for sale, he'd made it a surprise. When he wanted to tell her about the Cohens accepting the offer Lila had made on their behalf, he'd shown her a photo Lila had texted him of her putting an Under Contract sign on the property.

So whatever this was about, it wasn't something that would make her happy.

She sat down and braced herself. "What's up?"

"The captain assigned me a minor case today," he said.

Allie stared at him. Had she called this or what? Not good news. "But you're not even on the force yet! Not for two weeks!"

She didn't add the rush of worry she was feeling—that it was starting already. If he'd been assigned a case when he hadn't even started back yet, what would it be like come January?

"It's a minor burglary case in the neighborhood," he said. "Not a task force. Nothing dangerous."

"Oh," she said, her heart rate returning to normal. "But couldn't the captain have assigned it to a rookie?"

"He wants an experienced cop on it—he thinks there's something unusual about the case and wants to keep it on the down low until I can report back with more information on what I think is going on."

"Unusual? In what way?"

"A Christmas-present thief has stolen two gifts—marked with kids' names—from two houses on Oak Hill Road. I don't think it'll take much time. Are you okay with me doing a little investigating?"

"A present thief? Yikes," she said. "That is unusual. You know, maybe you working a light case before officially rejoining the PD is a good thing. A chance to transition back in while having a family this time around."

"That's a good way to look at it," he said.

What were the chances Theo would become obsessed with the Wedlock Creek Christmas-present snatcher and work all hours of the night, obsessing about catching the perpetrator? Very unlikely.

She thought, anyway. The old Theo had made it his mission to wrap up his cases.

He reached for her hand, and she looked down at their entwined fingers. "I know what you're thinking."

"You do?" she asked, wondering if he did. He'd always been very good at reading her mind. Reading *her.*

He grinned. "You're thinking that I'm going to catch the thief in no time and be focused on *your* Christmas present the way I should be."

She laughed. "That wasn't what I was thinking. But I prefer it, so let's go with that."

He held her gaze, his green eyes intense on her. "I made you a promise, Allie. I won't ever let my work come between us again."

When he looked at her that way, spoke with such

conviction, she believed him. Or did she just desperately want to?

Because truth be told, not losing him to his work was *really* what she wanted for Christmas.

Chapter Nine

The next morning, Theo rang the bell of 42 Oak Hill Road. A tall, thin man with silver-rimmed glasses answered the door. After introductions and handshakes, Michael Dumford led Theo to the scene of the crime: the family Christmas tree.

"We're last-minute shoppers," his wife, Carrie, said, "So we only had four presents under the tree so far. The one that's missing was a medium-size wrapped gift—a Lego set for our seven-year-old, Miles."

"And these three were left untouched," Theo said, jotting down some notes. "Were they moved, even slightly?"

Michael nodded. "Actually, yes, they all were. I'm quite a stickler for things being just so, and I'd arranged them by size on top of one another. The biggest box, containing a new snowsuit for Lucy, our three-year-old, then the Lego set on top of that, and then two wrapped packs of Pokemon cards on top of that. The Lego set was gone, the small gifts were just lying on the floor, and the big box was a few inches from where I'd placed it."

Huh. So the thief did some shaking and made some quick decisions. If you shook a Lego box, you pretty much knew what it was. They were on the pricey side, so it made sense the thief would go for that over a box that didn't move, which suggested a bulky clothing item.

"And nothing else was taken from the home?" Theo asked.

"We checked and double-checked," Mrs. Dumford said. "Nothing. There were even two twenty-dollar bills folded on top of that credenza," she added, pointing. "The money would have been in full view of the thief."

Interesting. Theo jotted that down. "What day did you notice the gift was missing?"

"It was two days ago. I happened to mention to Lolly Pfferman, four doors down, that the gift just vanished, and she mentioned that her neighbor, Ellen Gibson, also had a present go missing. So we both reported it to the police."

"Now, Mr. and Mrs. Dumford, I do have to ask this. Are you reasonably certain that your seven-year-old didn't take the gift? Unable to handle the suspense?"

Mr. Dumford smiled. "It was our first thought. But we asked him and unless he's a future Academy Award winner, he didn't take it. We also checked his room thoroughly. No sign of the Lego set or the wrapping paper. And trust me, I may be neat, but he's not. Even if he hid the ripped-off wrapping paper, bits of it would have been all over the place, including his hair."

Theo smiled. "And the thief could have just walked right in, no forced entry?"

"We tend to leave the back and side door unlocked during the day," Mrs. Dumford said. "I'm training our puppy and so I'm in and out of the yard with him all day."

"Can you recall if anyone other than family was in your home the day the gift went missing? Service worker?"

"No, no one," Mrs. Dumford said. "I went to pick up Miles from school—he's in second grade at Wedlock Creek Elementary—and I took him to karate and we stopped for smoothies. We were home by five thirty. And it was after dinner when Michael noticed the Lego set was gone."

Theo nodded. "Did you notice if the gift was there before you left to pick up Miles?"

She shook her head. "That I can't say. I just wasn't focused on the tree or the gifts right then."

Theo wrote down the time frame, then slid his little Moleskine notebook and pen back in his pocket. "Well, I think I've got what I need, for now. I'm going to take a look outside, check the entry points. And then I'll be in touch once I have some information."

This was an odd one. Someone had slipped in and picked and chosen, then made off with a decent-size wrapped gift. Why not take them all? Why just the one? Since a house several doors down was also targeted, the thief might be going slow to start, taking just one gift per house every couple of days to start. Since he or she had gotten away with it, Theo had no doubt that another theft or two would be reported today.

"Thank you, Sergeant Stark," Michael Dumford said, extending his hand.

Sergeant Stark. Damn, he liked the way that sounded. He hadn't been called that in almost two years. Not in an official-while-working-a-case capacity, anyway.

And not that he was official yet. He was just doing the captain a favor. He wouldn't be back on the force till January 2.

But being Sergeant Stark sure felt good. Maybe too good.

"You haven't had I'm-back sex? You're kidding!"

Allie made a face at her sister Lila, who was staring at her like she was completely nuts.

"No, I get it," her other sister, Merry, put in, taking a bite of the bruschetta Allie had made for the mini get-together. "They're waiting until it's right."

The MacDougal triplets sat on the sofa in the family room of Allie's house. Why had Allie opened her big fat mouth? Lila had simply asked how things were going between her and Theo, and like a fool, Allie had blurted out everything she was thinking and feeling. That was the problem with being so close to your sisters, she thought. You told them everything. And then they knew everything. Like the fact that she and her husband had barely kissed since his return.

"I did give him a foot massage," Allie said. "With lotion."

Lila shook her head sadly.

Even Merry, always levelheaded and thoughtful, winced.

"A foot massage," Lila repeated. She shook her head again. "That's it. I've had enough of this." She turned to Allie and pointed at her with her bruschetta, an errant tiny tomato falling off onto the coffee table. "You and Theo are going out tonight. Date night, isn't that what you marrieds call it? You're going out to a romantic restaurant—Merry and I are giving you a gift certificate to Marcello's."

"Oh, we are, are we?" Merry said, shaking her head on a laugh.

"Yes. And then they're coming home to a quiet house with no babies interrupting them from whatever may happen."

"She's pushy," Merry said, "but it's a good idea. You two haven't had a night alone since Theo came back. Maybe a little romance is exactly what you need."

"Oh, it is," Lila said.

Allie loved that Lila was still such a romantic. Her boyfriend of four years had recently broken up with her when Lila had been hoping for an engagement ring for Christmas. Merry was a serial dater, rarely going out with anyone twice. Once she'd said, *I'm looking for what you felt when you met Theo. You said the earth moved. I want the earth to move. And if there's not even a tremor on the first date, after three hours of a date, the earth's never going to move.*

Well, Allie didn't know about that. Lust could be a mystery. A friend of hers hadn't been remotely interested in a blind date but gave the guy another chance, and whammo, by date three, she was madly in love and couldn't believe she'd almost overlooked the guy for being "kind of nerdy." And Allie had never felt about any guy the way she had about Theo the day she'd met him. The senior cat she'd adopted from the shelter three days prior had slipped out the front door of the condo she'd been renting with her sisters and had run straight up a tree onto a branch and was sitting there, looking quite pleased with herself. She'd lived right on Main Street then and had been so worried Maisy would come down only to run right into the busy street. She'd been trying to coax the cat down by shaking a pouch of kitty treats, but Maisy just ignored her and surveyed the great outdoors.

A very good-looking guy, tall, dark-haired and green-eyed, was coming out of the coffee shop when he noticed her trying to persuade Maisy down and into her arms. He'd said, "Oh, I'll get her down for you," climbed up the tree like it was a ladder, gave Maisy a gentle scritch behind the ears and at the base of her tail. Her knight in sexy jeans had earned a rub along his arm from Maisy and been allowed to pick her up and carry her down. *My hero.* Allie wouldn't have been surprised if cartoon hearts were shooting out of her chest. She'd pointed out her front door, and her hero had rushed the cat over, opened the door, put her inside and closed the door. Eleven-year old Maisy was safe and sound. And Allie had herself a date with Theo Stark for that very night. *And* that night, she knew she would marry this man—or that she wanted to. The rest was history. Up-and-down history.

Maybe "date night" *was* what she and Theo needed. The two of them sitting across each other in a low-lit

Italian restaurant with those gorgeous oil paintings on the walls, a candle between them, some wine, some very good pasta, and returning home to an empty house with no responsibilities. That did sound good.

"You're sure you guys want to take the quads overnight?" Allie said, taking a sip of her iced tea. "One or two tend to wake up at least once." Merry was a teacher and would have to be at school early in the morning. Lila was a real estate broker whose busiest times were weekends.

"I don't have any showings till ten thirty," Lila said. "And I'll handle any middle-of-the-night wake-ups so Merry can get her beauty sleep. Those quads are ours. Till 10:00 a.m, anyway."

"There. So if you two have a very late night and want to sleep in tomorrow, Lila's got you covered till ten."

"Okay, and thank you," she told her sisters, feeling very lucky. "If Theo even wants to, that is."

Lila rolled her eyes. "Oh, please. Theo loves Italian food. And based on what you've said, he's not the one taking things boringly slow. That's on you."

Once again, all her fault for sharing every last detail of her love life or lack thereof with her sisters.

But she sure did get the warm fuzzies as she thought about herself and Theo ripping off each other's clothes when they got home. Yes, this idea of her sisters was sounding better and better.

And she did have a feeling Theo would like the idea of a date night.

"We want all the details, too," Lila said. "Nothing is too personal among triplets, right?"

Allie laughed. Apparently not.

* * *

The last time Allie and Theo had been in Marcello's was for their fifth anniversary, six months before that fateful night. Allie hadn't even been planning on a night out, given the state of their relationship in those days, but she was trying everything she could to get their marriage back on track, and a special dinner out to celebrate their first milestone seemed a good idea.

Theo had dressed up, looking especially gorgeous, and at first, as they'd clinked wineglasses and settled back to look over the menu, all was well. Then the texts had started from his captain and another sergeant. The case. Always the case. A witness reported seeing a tall, thin man with dark hair, ice-blue eyes and a jagged scar on his forehead, skulking around the back of a fast-food restaurant off the freeway coming into the town. McBruin. Theo, to his credit, hadn't bolted out of Marcello's, gun blazing. Instead, he'd sat there, looking miserable and uncomfortable, stuck at his anniversary dinner with his wife when he wanted to be hunting down a murderer. Theo had barely said two words, made some small talk in response to whatever Allie had said, and she could tell he was jumping out of his skin.

So, their entrees not even served yet, Allie had told him to just go, and he'd asked if she was sure, and she'd nodded, unable to speak lest she burst into tears. And he'd gone. She'd brought home their dinners in a doggie bag, and neither had touched the containers—Theo out of guilt, she was sure, and Allie from memory association, until Allie finally threw them away five days later.

Now here they were again, Allie trying to take Marcello's back for herself. She hadn't been able to step foot in the amazing Italian restaurant since that night. Now she had a chance to take a big step forward in her marriage and cross Marcello's off her banned list.

"You look so pretty, Allie," Theo said, his gaze on her across the table, candelight creating a soft glow.

"Thank you," she said, glad she'd worn the black jersey knee-length wrap dress Lila had insisted on as she'd gone through Allie's closet when she and Merry had returned with the gift certificate. Allie had been planning to wear pants and a pretty cardigan with a camisole underneath, but Lila had declared the outfit unworthy of date night and she and Merry had pawed through her closet, both agreeing on the black dress as the perfect blend of sexy, elegant and chic. "You look very handsome yourself." He wore all black, down to the tie imprinted with tiny silver circles.

He smiled. "I'm glad your sisters gave us the gift certificate. I owe them one. Dinner and overnight babysitting? I owe them big."

She smiled. "They're pretty great."

"They are." He took a sip of his red wine and leaned slightly forward. "Ah, I just got another hint of your perfume. I've missed it."

She'd wondered if he'd remember it. Chanel No. 19 was an old classic, but she loved it and it drove him wild, so it had been her signature scent. She hadn't worn it since that failure of an anniversary dinner two years ago. Tonight, she'd dabbed it behind her ears and in her cleavage.

He reached out a hand across the table, and she slid hers into it. "I also want you to know that my cell phone is in that stained glass bowl on our living room coffee table."

She could have gasped. "Really?"

He slightly lifted his arms. "A pat-down would reveal I'm telling the truth."

She laughed. "I believe you."

Huh. No phone. That was big. It meant he was *more* than just trying.

Then again, he wasn't on the force yet. There were no cases—well, no big cases. No emergency calls. Now that she thought about it, leaving his phone behind wasn't exactly a big deal.

"I know what you're thinking," he said, putting down his menu.

Fully decided on the lemon piccata, she, too, put aside the menu. "What am I thinking?"

"That it was hardly a struggle to leave my phone, given I haven't started back at the PD."

She smiled. "Busted. Both of us."

"But," he said, taking a piece of Italian bread from the basket, "I did do some investigating today on the Christmas-present thief case. I have to say, it did feel good being back on the job."

She reached for his hand and gave it a squeeze. "I know how much you love being a cop, Theo. I hope you know I don't want to take that away from you. You do know that, right?"

"Of course, I know that."

"Good. So what's the story on the present thief? Can you talk about it?"

"I met with both families today. The first family targeted had a Lego set stolen. The second family had a pricey art set taken."

"A Lego set and pastels?" Allie said. "What kind of thief is this?"

"Either someone who can't afford to buy Christmas presents for his own children, or the thief *is* a kid."

"Either way, that's heartbreaking," Allie said.

He nodded and was about to say something, but the server appeared, listing the specials. Allie stuck with the lemon piccata and Theo ordered the always irresistible chicken parmigiana.

"The victims have teenagers?" she asked as the server left.

"Nope, young kids. No older than seven. In fact, each home targeted had a seven-year-old. I'm not sure if that factors in yet, but it might."

"Merry teaches second grade at the elementary school. You could talk to her and see if there are any connections between them."

"I'll do that," he said. He sipped his wine. "You don't mind talking shop?"

"I actually always loved talking about your cases. All kinds. I love knowing how your mind works to figure things out. That was never the issue."

"I know," he said. "I hate what I did the last time we were here, Allie. In fact, I'm surprised you even wanted to go here tonight."

"I'm taking the place back for myself. For us. It's the only way to conquer something."

He smiled and held her gaze. "I'm glad we're here. I'm glad we're celebrating."

"What are we celebrating?" she asked, suddenly wanting to know how he saw it.

"That rare thing called a second chance. I've got one with you, and I'm not blowing it."

Tears stung the backs of her eyes and she sipped her wine to regain control of her emotions. The last thing she needed tonight was raccoon tracks down her face.

"That means everything to me, Theo."

A loud gasp followed by "Oh, my God. Yes! Yes! I will marry you" came from across the restaurant. Allie looked over, and a guy was getting up from his bent knee, his date gaping at the diamond ring sparkling on her finger.

Allie smiled and clapped along with the rest of the patrons. Theo let out a wolf whistle.

"I was thinking of proposing to you here," he said. "But this place didn't mean anything to us back then. It was just a fancy restaurant."

"I know what you mean," she said, remembering how he'd surprised her outside her condo, right under the beautiful tree where they'd met for the first time, where he'd rescued Maisy. They'd been dating for six months and were about to leave on a weekend camping trip. Under that tree, he'd pulled a velvet ring box from his pocket, gotten down on one knee and told her he loved her and wanted to spend the rest of his life with her and would she marry him. Allie had screamed much like the young woman had across the restaurant.

"I love that tree," she said. "It's a great excuse to get treats from the bakery that opened up right next to the condo so that I can visit the tree."

"You visit the tree?" he asked as the waiter set down their entrees.

Allie admired her lemon piccata and breathed in the delicious aroma. "Yup. When you first…left," she said, "I avoided it like the ole plague. I couldn't handle seeing it. In those first months, I was in such a daze that I didn't even know where I was half the time. My sisters would realize we were heading in that direction and they'd make elaborate detours so I could avoid it."

"Your sisters are awesome," he said.

She smiled. "Yeah, they are."

"And I really do owe them big for sending us here tonight."

"We'll bring them Marcello's amazing tiramisu. That'll make them both very happy." She eyed his entree, her mouth watering. "Your chicken parm looks amazing. I need at least four bites of that."

"You can have the first," he said, cutting a piece and holding it out toward her.

She leaned forward and tried to take the bite as sexily as possible, but hot mozzarella cheese and marinara sauce didn't make that possible. "Mmm, so good," she said. She cut a piece of her lemon piccata and held it out for him. He kept his gaze on hers as he wrapped those lips around the fork.

"Ah, that's delicious," he said.

And then they spent the next twenty minutes eating and talking and laughing and reminiscing, both howling over stories from that crazy camping trip the weekend he'd proposed, when they'd been stalked by a crazed wolf who turned out to be a scared and very sweet stray dog. They'd brought the adorable gray-and-black girl home and Allie's sisters had fallen so in love with the little mutt that Allie and Theo had handed her over. "Maisy would hate me anyway if I brought this one home," Allie had said. Now the once-skinny stray was named Josie, had five memory-foam pet beds in every room in her sisters' condo and had her own containers of dog ice cream in their freezer.

"I'll give you another foot massage for another bite of your chicken parm," Allie said.

"Deal," he said, holding out a bite.

"Sergeant Stark," a middle-aged woman said as she was about to pass their table with her husband. She stopped, just staring at Theo.

Theo looked up at her, clearly waiting for her to continue, but the woman didn't say anything, and if Allie wasn't mistaken, she was holding back tears.

"It's all right, dear," her husband said, putting his hands on her shoulders. "It's okay."

What was this? Allie wondered.

Theo stood and wrapped the woman in a silent hug. The woman nodded and took her husband's hand and they left.

"What was that about?" Allie asked.

"Tough incident regarding her son. He was early twenties at the time. Let's just say there were drugs involved and a bridge and now he's in college, volunteering at a crisis help line."

"Oh, Theo," she said. "You saved him?"

"He *wanted* to be saved. That made the difference. Not me."

She swallowed. "You never told me about that."

"There's a lot I don't bring home. Experiences I can't

handle talking about, especially right afterward. That night—just a couple weeks before I left two years ago—was a close call. It took a while to get him to safety."

She took a deep breath. "We'll find a middle ground. That's what it's about. Middle ground. You're you and it's why I love you. You're a cop."

"And you're a woman who wants her husband in her life, not an hour or two a week. I get that. I didn't before."

"We'll find our way," she said. "Because like you just said about that woman's son—we both *want* it. That's the difference. We *want* this second chance."

He reached out a hand and she took it and squeezed. She'd never felt so hopeful.

"I keep expecting to hear a 'waah!'" Theo said as they took their wine and the cookies Allie had baked this morning into the living room. They sat on the sofa, Theo loosening his tie.

"Me, too. And I keep forgetting that they're not here at all, so every now and then my heart stops with 'The quads! I left them alone in the family room!'"

Theo laughed. "That happened to me twice already." He sipped his wine, then plucked a cookie from the plate on the coffee table. "What's this?" he asked, eyeing the magazine folded open.

Allie felt her cheeks burn. Her sisters had "accidentally" left the magazine when they'd dropped off the gift certificate to Marcello's earlier. Accidentally with a neon-orange sticky note sticking up. "Oh, just some silly quiz my sisters think we should take. One of those

'Does your marriage need spicing up?' kinds of things." She shook her head. "So silly."

He picked up the magazine and said, "'Number one. What do you and your husband wear to sleep? A) Flannel pajamas—come on, it's winter! B) Comfy sweats—the older the better. C) Our birthday suits—to generate our own body heat. D) Something sexy that gets pulled off fast.'" He laughed. "Well, that's easy," he said, wagging a finger between them. "When we got home, we both immediately changed into something a lot more comfortable. So the correct answer is B) Comfy sweats."

Well, technically, changing had been Theo's idea. The second he'd stepped inside the house, he took off his jacket and loosened another button on his shirt. "Why don't we change and then we'll pick a movie and make a big bowl of popcorn," he'd said.

Change? she'd thought. Out of her sexy wrap dress? She liked how it made her feel. But Theo had been halfway up the stairs already. By the time she followed him up, he had grabbed his favorite army sweats and a flannel shirt and was heading into the bathroom.

Because despite being married, they didn't change in front of each other. Was that a question in the quiz? She hoped so.

Now, instead of her romance-inspiring date-night dress, she was wearing gray-and-white-striped yoga pants and a long pale pink tank top. Super sexy. Not.

But all hope of romance for tonight was not lost. Because Theo Stark was taking a *Cosmo* quiz. Would wonders never cease?

"Wait," he said. "I want to change my answer. These

yoga pants and tank tops that you always wear to bed? I have to admit, Allie—they do make me want to rip them off you."

She actually felt herself blush. They did? Who knew? "I actually find your army sweats very sexy. And you have one black T-shirt in particular..." Oh, God, what was she saying?

He started unbuttoning his flannel shirt, then took it off. "This one?" he asked.

Her mouth went dry as she stared at his chest covered in that fitted T-shirt, his biceps. She had to lick her lips in order to speak. "Yes, that one."

And before she could think about it or stop herself, she ran a hand up his arm, on that incredible, hard bicep, then the other.

"If I don't kiss you right now, I might have to go run ten miles or something," he said.

She leaned her face toward his and that was it—he kissed her, softly, then more passionately, grasping her face in his hands. One hand slid around her back, pulling her closer against him, the other lingering on the hem of her tank top. He was waiting for her to back away or say *That's not a good idea* or *Let's take this one step at a time*. But she said nothing and up the top went, over her bra (which she hadn't changed from her date-night choice) and over her head. Her yoga pants followed on the floor.

He took in her lacy black bra and matching underwear and groaned. She straddled him and pulled up the T-shirt, her hands exploring his chest that she was so familiar with. He flung the T-shirt off him, then lay her down on the sofa, kissing her, his hands in her hair, and suddenly they were both naked.

He reached for his wallet, which had fallen from his pants pocket onto the floor, and held up a little foil packet. "Unless you want twins or triplets?" he said. "Multiples clearly run in your family."

She laughed. "No, I'm all set for kids."

"Do you know that there's a detective on the force who married a woman with triplets and then they had twins a year later?" he asked, trailing kisses along her collarbone.

Ah, yes. The Barellis, she thought, her eyes fluttering closed as his lips moved north, then south, his hands moving aside the lacy bra. She knew Norah, who taught a class on newborn multiples at the community center. "That could be us," she said, then shook her head.

He kissed her again. "Exactly. Or *not*."

"Or not, for sure."

And then for the first time in almost two years, Allie Stark and her husband made love.

Chapter Ten

The problem with knowing your husband so well, even after a two-year hiatus, was that when he went quiet, you knew there was a problem.

Crud.

Allie's heart sank. At the moment, she was snuggled up against him in their bed, still naked, her head on his chest. For the last few minutes, they'd both been catching up on their breathing, coming back to earth after amazing sex, Theo on his back, looking up at the ceiling with pure satisfaction on his gorgeous face. Then she'd said something about how all her dreams seemed to be coming true.

That was it; the turning point from bliss on Theo's face to...something she couldn't quite put her finger on.

He stiffened beside her, turned his head slightly away and basically left the building.

Too much, too soon?

The sex? Talking about dreams coming true? The intimacy?

Grrrr! This was the whole reason she'd been afraid to do this, to get too close to him too soon. Because one of them wouldn't be ready. She'd thought that person was her, and so she'd gone for it. Guess what? It wasn't her!

"Everything okay?" she asked. *Say what's on your mind*, she reminded herself. *It has to be your mantra.*

"Everything's okay," he said, kissing the top of her head.

But he didn't say anything else, and because she could be chatty and start rambling and babbling about stuff that had nothing to do with what was poking at her, she forced herself to hold her tongue and just be quiet.

He's just processing, she told herself.

And so she kept her head on his chest whether it made him uncomfortable or not and closed her eyes. She'd give him the emotional space he seemed to need right now, but not physical space. She needed to be close to him right now, and if he was going to emotionally distance himself, then tough noogies that she was a barnacle right now.

"I think I hear one of the babies," he said and got out of bed. He was out the door before she could even think, *Nope, not one made a peep.*

Because the quads aren't home, Theo. They're at my sisters' for the night.

Allie sighed and flopped over in bed.

One step forward, half a step back. That was only a half step behind, then. Not so bad.

Really? This was how she was rationalizing what was happening? She shook her head at herself.

Then again, finding their way back to each other would take time, especially because there was no *there* there. *Back*, actually, was all wrong. What they had, even two years ago, was love, chemistry and history—all good, yes, but they'd wanted different things, different big things. What they had now was a family and a commitment to not wasting this second chance.

So let him do this at his pace, even if it's frustratingly glacial, she told herself. *He'll get there.* Seventy-five percent of her believed that. Twenty-five, though, had been there, done that and truly wasn't sure.

A cry woke Theo at just before 4:00 a.m. He waited fifteen seconds, per his baby-rearing book, to give whichever quad the opportunity to "self-soothe," using the time to soak in how lovely his wife looked, her pink-red lips slightly open, her blond hair half covering her beautiful face.

Then he remembered the babies weren't even here. He couldn't have heard a cry, just like he hadn't when he'd used it as an excuse to flee the bedroom not five minutes after they'd had sex.

With Allie snuggled against him right afterward, her head on his chest, he'd had the sudden urge to get away, to go out for a ten-mile run. His chest, his neck, the muscles in his legs had tightened to the point that he'd been physically uncomfortable.

What had that been about?

The more she snuggled and ran her hands up and down his chest, talking about how her dreams were coming true, the quieter he'd gotten. Suddenly, all he could think about was screwing up, choosing another complicated case over Allie, over his family, and he felt like he couldn't breathe. He kept saying he wouldn't let her down. But when she put it all there the way she had, he'd…panicked. He'd gone to the nursery and just sat in the glider, holding the rabbit puppet that had been on the seat, trying to get a grip. He wanted this. He wanted a second chance. He wanted his family. So what the hell was wrong with him?

When he'd finally returned to the bedroom, thinking about just telling her the truth, that he was scared spitless of ruining this beautiful, fledging thing between them, she was either asleep or pretending to be. And he'd been relieved to not have to say anything, so he'd gotten into bed, kissed her on the cheek and turned over. And hadn't slept for a good, long time.

Now, wide-awake at 4:00 a.m., he realized it was his own racing mind that had woken him up.

"Can't sleep?" Allie asked, tucking a swath of hair behind her ear.

He glanced at her. "Sorry I woke you."

"I've been tossing and turning all night," she said. "So it was about time for me to be awake anyway."

Knife to the heart. She couldn't sleep because of him! And he had no doubt she'd been unable to sleep since the night he didn't come home. He closed his eyes for a moment, then looked at her, wanting to take away the hurt and confusion in her expression. Hurt and confusion he'd put there after something so beautiful between them.

"Craziest thing," he said. "I thought I heard one of the babies crying again. Like earlier tonight."

"Earlier tonight you stayed in the nursery for over twenty minutes."

So she had been pretending to sleep. That she'd felt the need to do that said a lot about how tied up in knots he'd made her. This wasn't how he wanted things to go or be. But how to fix this when he wasn't sure what was going on with him?

"I do some of my best thinking in there," he said. "Something about the cribs with their names, the sun-and-moon rug, the glider chair, that rabbit puppet. Just being in that nursery helps me put things into perspective, prioritize."

"I know what you mean," she said and squeezed his hand.

The hand squeeze told him she was letting this go, that she knew he had to process some mumbo-jumbo for whatever reason, and she was giving him time and room. She could have told him off and rightly so, how he'd pretty much ruined great sex because it was all too much, too close, too this, too that. But she didn't tell him off. She'd squeezed his hand.

He turned over onto his stomach and faced her, but she stayed on her back, looking straight ahead. "So what time are we picking up the quads from Lila and Merry's?"

"Not till ten. So we should try to get some sleep. The quads won't care if we're exhausted tomorrow."

He smiled. "Right?"

"Actually, I just remembered that Lila wanted some girl time, so I'll pick up the kiddos on my own. Maybe we can meet for lunch?"

He held her gaze for a moment and knew immediately that Lila didn't need girl time. His wife did. To talk about *him*.

"Everything okay with Lila?" he asked, pulling the comforter up to his chest. He figured he'd give her the chance to talk in code. As in: *No, because her dear sister is trying to make a real go of her marriage to her not-dead husband, who's pulling away just when he's reeled her in.*

"Just some romance woes. We all have them."

"We'll be okay, Allie," he said, stroking her hair. "This is all brand-new. Sort of."

She laughed, thank God. "*Sort of* is right. And we have one question of a *Cosmo* quiz to thank for getting us into bed together. Naked."

And then he'd gone and ruined it by feeling his collar squeezing his neck when he was buck naked.

"So Lila is having romance woes?" he asked.

"She's had some blind dates. All disasters."

"You should send Josie up the tree in front of her condo and then Mr. Right will pass by and climb up to save the mutt for her."

She smiled a bittersweet smile. "Dogs can't climb trees."

I'm sorry I'm so bad at this, he wanted to say. *That I don't know how to be the husband you need. That everything feels so strange and so right at the same time.*

"She'll be okay," Allie said, but she didn't sound so sure.

When she turned over, facing away from him, he spooned beside her and put his arm around her. A second later, she wrapped her hand around his arm.

Maybe they really would be okay, too. He sure hoped so.

"So…?" Lila asked the minute she let Allie into her condo. "Please don't tell me Merry and I spent a hundred bucks on a Marcello's gift certificate for nothing."

Josie, the adorable gray-and-black mixed breed that she and Theo had brought home from that camping trip seven years ago, came over and Allie kneeled down to give her a good scratching behind the ears and a cuddle, then stood up and gave her sister a soft punch in the arm. "No matter what, it wouldn't have been a waste because we got you dessert to-go with the leftover money. Their tiramisu is out of this world."

"Oooh, thanks," Lila said, taking the bag into the kitchen and putting it in the fridge.

"Babies asleep?" Allie asked into the quiet. "Tail end of their nap?"

"Yes, which means you have a good fifteen minutes to tell me every detail of last night." She went to the cabinet and pulled out two mugs, filling them with coffee. Allie went to the fridge to get the half-and-half and plunked some in. Josie padded in and curled up in the blue plush bed by the window.

"I'll make you a deal, Allie. If you tell me, I'll give you half my tiramisu. I can't speak for Merry and her tiramisu, since she's at work."

Allie smiled. "Deal," she said, sitting down and stirring a spoonful of sugar in her coffee.

Lila took out one of the tiramisus and brought over two spoons. Allie took a bite and savored the cool, sweet perfection. It was so good it almost made her feel better.

"Marcello's worked," Allie said. "You and Merry taking the quads worked."

Lila's face lit up and she spooned a mouthful of the dessert into her mouth. "And it was amazing, right? Told you! You two just needed a night to yourselves with romance on the menu as your dessert."

"Dinner was amazing. *Dessert* was amazing. It was afterward that wasn't amazing." Allie took a heaping spoonful of tiramisu. "I think I scared him off by saying something about my dreams coming true."

Lila put her spoon down with a little clang. "Scared him off? What is he, sixteen? A guy you're dating? Give me an effing break, Allie."

"I know. It sounds stupid. But we had big problems in our marriage toward the end. You know that. And we were apart for two years. In a way, it does feel like we're dating—finding out who we are together, if we work—"

"Wait, *if*? What?"

Allie burst into tears, grabbing tissues from the box on the counter. "He wants us to work. I want us to work. But what if the chasm was too deep and too far? I know Theo. I know what he's worried about."

Lila narrowed her blue eyes. "What is he worried about?"

"That he'll revert back to Sergeant Stark. That he'll put the job above me and his children. That it'll be the same thing all over again except this time he'll break five hearts instead of just one."

"Oh, crud," Lila said. "I kind of get it."

"I get it, too. I don't like it, but I get it."

"So when he starts on the force, he's out chasing a mobster or whatever and you text him to pick up a loaf of organic whole-grain bread on his way home, and not only does he not come home till 1:00 a.m., he forgets the bread. And then you have a fight that wakes up the babies, and they're crying, then you're both crying, and two nights later, the same thing happens?"

Allie's shoulders slumped and she took another bite of her tiramisu. "Exactly."

"He has to find a middle ground," Lila said. "Plain and simple. He's not the only cop on the force with a family. Look at Reed Barelli. He's got five kids—toddler triplets and baby twins! God, can you imagine?"

Allie smiled. "Theo took the quads on a playdate with Reed and his twins. They have very good systems in place."

"Yes, systems that keep Detective Barelli from following leads and tips all over the night, guns blazing in abandoned warehouses. Theo has the same reason to change how he operates—a family to think about."

"Then why is Theo even worried?" Allie asked. And why did she think her sister possibly knew her husband better than she did?

"Because so much is riding on him doing this right. He wants to be a cop. He's good at it. It was his life for years. Now you and the kids are his life. He has to make the two work. And he has some time before he even rejoins the force to think about it, make decisions—and to freak out about making the wrong ones."

Allie shoved the rest of the tiramisu in her mouth. Her sister was too right. "If you're not going to finish that…" she said, gesturing at what was left in her sister's dish.

Lila smiled. "You two are going through the hard part right now. Forging your way. Everything will work out, I know it. Like you said before, Allie—you both want this second chance. That's what matters. What you'll both do to make sure it's not thrown away."

"Wait, what we'll *both* do? Are you saying I have to compromise, too?" She gave Lila a devilish smile and dipped her spoon in her sister's cup.

"Name of the game," Lila said. "Wow, I should be a marriage counselor. I'm pretty good at this."

"You are," Allie said, giving Lila a little bow.

Lila laughed. "Too bad I'm showing a half-million-dollar house with mountain views in thirty minutes, or I'd think about it. Oh, and the fact that I'm divorced and have one meh blind date after another. The other night's guy texted someone for a full two minutes right after our entrees were served and it felt ill-mannered for me to start eating when he was 'otherwise engaged,' so I waited." She shook her head. "Forget me as a therapist. I would have counseled myself to take my plate of lemon sole and overturn it on his head."

"You should have. I would have loved to see that."

Lila laughed. "Do you believe he asked me out again? By *text*! Some people, right?"

Allie laughed so hard that Josie came over to investigate. She gave the dog a hug, rubbing her sides. "Remember when you were a scared little stray in the woods, Jo-Jo? Look at you now. Memory-foam bed, squeaky toys and rawhide bones aplenty."

Josie licked her hand, then padded back over to her bed and curled up.

"Waah! Waah-waah!" came cries from across the condo.

"Not one but two baby Starks announcing they've awakened from their naps," Lila said. She got up and went charging into the den, where there were four port-a-cribs. The room looked like a mini nursery. Her sisters were the world's greatest aunts. "Fi, fi, fo, fum, I smell the diaper of a quadruplet-man."

"Could be Olivia," Allie said with a smirk.

"Nope, because I dealt with Miss Olivia right before their naps. Definitely quadruplet-*man*."

Allie laughed and went to the port-a-cribs. "Yup, it's Henry. Oh," she said, pinching her nose. "And Tyler." Olivia stirred and sat up, followed by Ethan.

"A mom's and aunt's work is never done," Lila said, scooping up Henry while Allie picked up Tyler. "So what's the plan for today?" she asked, sprinkling cornstarch on Henry's tush.

"I'm meeting Theo for lunch at the Pie Diner at noon and we'll spend the day together."

"Good. Everything will be fine," Lila said. "It really will."

When her sister said it, with such conviction as she put Henry in his winter bunting and into the stroller, reaching for the next quad, Allie believed it.

Chapter Eleven

Theo arrived at the Pie Diner, one of his favorite lunch spots, but Allie and the quads weren't there yet. He saw a few of his fellow officers from the PD at the counter, including Detective Reed Barelli, whose wife's family owned the place. He stopped and said hello, then headed to a big table in the back and asked for four high chairs.

"Did you say four?" the waitress asked, gaping at him.

Arlena Ingalls, the owner and Reed Barelli's mother-in-law, grinned at the waitress, then at Theo. "Today's her first day and she's new to town. Hasn't gotten used to all the multiples. By tomorrow, she'll ask how many high chairs before she even asks how many in the party."

Theo smiled. "Welcome to Wedlock Creek. My wife and baby quads will be here any minute."

"Baby quads," the waitress said with wonder. "Wow."

"Won't faze you in a few days," Arlena said to the young woman. "My neighbor has three sets of twins."

"And people do this on purpose," Theo added. "They marry at the Wedlock Creek Wedding Chapel because of its legend."

The waitress shivered. "Well, I do hope to find my Mr. Right, but keep me away from that chapel! I want two kids, two years apart, a boy, then a girl."

Arlena laughed. "You'll have quintuplets without even stepping foot in the chapel. That's how life works."

"Don't say that!" the waitress said with wide eyes, then hurried over to refill a glaring customer's coffee.

"True, right?" Theo said to Arlena. "Take your son-in-law over there. Came to town a bachelor cop, very same day found himself married and the father of triplet babies. Because of the Wedlock Creek Chapel. I don't believe in that kind of superstitious stuff usually, but evidence *is* walking and crawling all over town. And I should know—*I* got married there."

Arlena grinned. "And it sure is good for business. Those little multiples grow up and want their potpie."

Theo glanced around and took in several patrons who looked a lot alike. One day, his kids would be having lunch in here on a weekend or after school. The thought made him smile. His kids, teenagers. That seemed like a million years away, but he knew that time would come in the blink of an eye.

He looked toward the door. No sign of Allie and the quads yet. It wasn't quite noon, so he took out his Moleskine notebook and flipped through his notes on the present-thief case. This morning he'd gotten a call from the captain that two more houses had been targeted yesterday, this time on Willow Road, which ran perpendicular to Oak Hill. He'd paid a visit to one of the homes—same story. A gift with their seven-year-old son's name on it had been swiped. Four other gifts with other family members' names—left untouched. Also not taken was an iPod on the coffee table right near the Christmas tree.

The thief seemed interested in taking only one gift per home and marked for a seven-year-old boy, regardless of who that boy was. Actually, scratch that. So far, three of the boys (he couldn't meet with the other homeowners on Willow Road until this afternoon) did have something in common besides their age: they were all in the same class at Wedlock Creek Elementary. And Allie's sister Merry was a teacher at that school. He'd give her a call after he met with the fourth victim to get her teacherly take on the situation, then he'd meet with the teacher of the second-grade class.

The thief was looking more and more like a seven-year-old. No forced entry. None of the neighbors noticed anyone strange lurking around. Nothing of value, besides a gift, taken from any of the homes. Of course, at this point, Theo couldn't be sure they were dealing with a pint-sized burglar whose getaway mode of transportation was likely a two-wheeler with a basket. But it was a very strong possibility.

His phone pinged with a text: Can we skip lunch? Henry's screechy and Olivia is having a monster tantrum. See you for dinner at 6 at home?

Hmm. Interesting. She wasn't asking him to come home to help out with the screeching and the tantrum.

She was making it pretty clear she'd just see him for dinner later.

He signaled the new waitress. "You can take away the high chairs. Turns out it's just me. And in fact, I'll go join the guys at the counter."

She smiled and removed the high chairs, stacking them in her arms.

"On your own for lunch after all?" Arlena asked, grabbing a pencil from behind her ear and taking out her order pad.

On his own. Interesting how he didn't like the sound of that. He nodded, taking a seat next to Officer Gronkowsky. "I'd love the buffalo chicken potpie. And a refill of my club soda."

"Coming right up," she said.

For the next ten minutes, he talked and joked with his fellow officers, none of whom talked shop in public, of course, and it was great shooting the ole breeze with this group, most of whom he'd known for years. Two he hadn't known two years ago—Detective Barelli and Monkler, a rookie. But it felt damned good to be sitting with his peeps, who understood without saying a word.

After the best potpie he could remember having, Theo settled up and said goodbye to the officers, who were heading back to the PD. In his car, he called Mandy Pearlman and asked if now would be a good time for him to meet with her about the gift stolen from her home. She wasn't available until two thirty, so he killed some time by going over his notes and driving through the neighborhood where all the thefts took place.

At just before two thirty, he parked his car on the street and tried to envision the perp-kid's path. The kid came from left or right on his bike, zipped in through the driveway and beyond to the side door, found it unlocked—which was often the case in Wedlock Creek—slid in, looked under the tree for a gift marked for a kid in his class, ran out, stuffed the gift in his basket, covered it with a towel or something like that and made off.

Suddenly it didn't seem so likely. How would a seven-year-old know no one was home? How had he gotten lucky in that department four times? How could no one have seen him run out with the gift?

All the thefts were known to have happened between three and five thirty in the afternoon, which made the seven-year-old theory more plausible. Those were prime kid hours for playing after school, riding bikes, even in December. It was cold out, but the streets and sidewalks were clear of snow. The other house targeted on this street was just a few doors up. And the other two houses were just around the corner.

The thief lived in the neighborhood. Two houses a street? Perhaps Redwood Road, which opened from Oak Hill, would be next. A stakeout might be in order tomorrow at 3:00 p.m.

He got out of his truck and headed up the porch steps to 45 Willow. A little girl with two red braids opened the door, her mother behind her.

"You're not a policeman," the girl said with a frown. "Mommy said a policeman was here."

Theo kneeled on the doorstep. "Actually, I am a police officer. I'm just not in my uniform right now." He was about to pull his badge from his pocket to show her, then remembered he didn't have it back yet.

"Oh," the girl said. "Somebody stole my brother's ant farm and it was supposed to be from me." Tears misted her eyes.

"I'm very sorry about that," Theo said. "Tell you what. I have some questions to ask your mom and then I'll do my best to catch the thief."

"Hi, I'm Mandy Pearlman," her mother said, extending her hand. She turned to the girl. "Sweetie, why don't you go play quietly in your room while I talk to the policeman, okay?"

The girl scampered off, and Theo followed Mrs. Pearlman into the living room. He sat across from her on a love seat facing a sofa. The Christmas tree was in front of the window.

"Why don't you start with when you noticed the gift was missing from under the tree?" Theo said.

"It was just after five o'clock. I'd just gotten home with the kids—I'd picked up my seven-year-old and then he had a karate class. The minute the kids ran through the door, they went straight for the tree to see if any new presents were there. With only a week to go till Christmas, they're a little obsessed."

"Understandable." *Karate class.* Something poked at his memory, and he flipped back in his notebook. Yup, there it was. Three other seven-year-olds were also in karate and had been at the class with either mom or dad when the thefts likely occurred.

And who would know who had karate on what days? A kid in their class.

"We're the fourth house that's been robbed," Mrs. Pearlman said. "Are you close to catching the burglar?"

"I have a solid lead," he said. "I expect to have the

case wrapped up by tomorrow at the latest. I can't guarantee that, of course. In the meantime, please keep your doors locked when you're not at home."

"Sergeant Stark, I certainly hope you're not blaming the victim!" Mrs. Pearlman said, lifting her chin.

Whoa. "Of course not. I just want to make it harder for the thieves, that's all."

She raised an eyebrow. "Well, there was a time when you didn't have to lock your doors in Wedlock Creek."

He nodded and flipped his notebook closed, then stood up. "I'll be in touch," he said and almost added a *ma'am*, but she was riled up enough.

He glanced at his watch. It was just after 3:00 p.m. Perhaps his sister-in-law Merry would be free to talk. Back in his truck, he pulled out his phone and called Wedlock Creek Elementary and asked for Merry MacDougal.

"What can I do for you, Theo?" his sister-in-law asked. "And thanks for the tiramisu, by the way. Lila texted me a picture of it earlier. Hopefully she didn't eat mine, too."

He laughed. "Least we could do, considering you paid for it. Listen, I'm calling about something sensitive, potentially involving a second-grade student at Wedlock Creek Elementary. Can we meet?"

"Yikes. Why don't you come over to the school right now? It's past three, but most of the teachers will be here for a while, grading and lesson planning, if you need to talk to the second-grade teachers."

"Great. I'll see you in about ten minutes."

When Theo arrived at Wedlock Creek Elementary, students were running around the playground, filing into buses and being picked up by parents. It was quite possible that the pint-sized Sticky Hands was preparing his bike right now for another present swipe. But there was no karate class today, so likely the thief would take today off.

After he was buzzed in, Theo checked in with the school secretary and then took the stairs to the second level. He walked down the hall of the fourth-grade wing, smiling at the self-portraits lining the walls. In room 412, he found Ms. MacDougal putting a star on a math sheet. She put the paper in a file folder and then turned to him. “Please tell me it’s nothing serious, Theo. I’ve been sitting here grading that same math sheet for the past ten minutes.”

He told her about the case, her shoulders slumping with each sentence.

“Based on the names of two siblings I have in my class, I think the seven-year-olds you mentioned are all in Mrs. Finley’s class. She’s in room 202.”

He double-checked his notes. “All four are. So it does sound to you like we have a second-grade thief on our hands?” Theo asked.

Merry nodded. “Unfortunately.” She picked up her cell phone and pressed in a number. “Jen? Do you have a few minutes? My brother-in-law, Theo, is working a case right now for the PD and he’d like to speak to you.” She listened for a moment. “Well, it might involve a child in your class. He’ll be right down.”

“Thanks,” Theo said and headed down the hall, down the stairs, to the right, to the left and to room 202. This place was a mini maze.

He explained the case to Jen Finley, whose shoulders also slumped like Merry's had.

"Oh, dear," she said. She took out a schedule book. "There are seven students who take karate after school. Five boys and three girls. Oh, wait, four boys and three girls. One stopped taking the class about a week ago."

A week ago. Right around when the first thefts occurred.

"Do you know why?" Theo asked.

"It's very sad," the teacher said. "Hunter Chadwell's father died three months ago, and things have been tough financially on his mother."

"That's very rough on a kid," Theo said. "Hunter Chadwell is in this class?"

She nodded.

"Does he happen to live in the Oak Hill neighborhood?"

"He does. He lives right on Oak Hill Road."

"Have you ever seen him ride a bike with a basket?"

"Not a basket, but a crate attached to the back."

Ah, like when Theo was a kid. "Why don't we keep this quiet until I have a chance to talk to Hunter's mom and interview him myself? He's just a possibility at this point. Not even a suspect. I just have some decent circumstantial evidence."

"Mum's the word," she said.

With the name and address of a seven-year-old "possibility" in his notebook, Theo left the school feeling like absolute crud.

Not meeting Theo for lunch was part of Operation Give Theo Space. Olivia had truly had a monster tantrum, but she'd come out of it with fifteen minutes to spare, and Allie could have gotten the group to the Pie Diner to meet him, as planned. But the baby girl was still slightly out of sorts and Allie did think Theo could use a little breathing room.

Of course, no sooner had that thought come to her than another one had: he'd had almost two years of breathing room.

But she was dealing with the now. And if letting Theo go about his life in Wedlock Creek with a bit of distance after last night would make him more comfortable, then fine. She would.

She had plenty to do herself.

Such as cook for her client Virginia Gelman. Allie used the quads' afternoon nap to get started on the meal for Virginia, this time for a small dinner party at her home. She'd asked for the very time-intensive beef bourguignon that had to taste exactly like Julia Child's. According to Virginia, her very "judgy" sister-in-law and husband were coming for dinner, so the meal had to be Julia-perfect and no one could know Virginia hadn't made it herself. The pot of beef, bacon and vegetables in the wine and stock had been cooking in the oven for almost four hours. The small kitchen had always been fine for Allie's needs as a personal chef, but she couldn't wait to get into that dream kitchen in the new house.

Remember that, she told herself. They would be starting fresh in a new home, a family home. Their forever home.

She'd just started sautéing the pearl onions in butter and slicing the mushrooms when she heard Theo opening the front door. As always, her heart skipped a beat.

"Wow, that smells amazing," he said as he walked into the kitchen. "So amazing it's all I can think about, and for that, I'm grateful."

"Well, the bad news is that the beef bourguignon I'm making isn't for us—it's for Virginia Gelman's dinner party. But I'm glad it's taken your mind off something bad. Is it the Christmas-present case?"

He nodded. "Looks like our thief is a little boy in second grade."

"Oh, no," she said. "Are you sure?"

"Not a hundred percent, but it sure looks that way. I'll tell you all about it tomorrow once it's a sure thing." He sniffed the air again. "Sure I can't steal some of that?"

"I did make extra," she said, "for not only seconds but thirds. I could give you a tiny bit."

He smiled. "I don't want to get you in trouble with Virginia Gelman. That woman is fierce."

She added the mushrooms to the skillet of onions. "How about if I make it for us tomorrow?"

"Deal. What can I do for you?"

She thought about that. *You could give me last night, take two, but with a different ending.*

What came out of her mouth was "You can stay home with the quads while I deliver this to Virginia."

"Win-win. I miss the Starklets," he said. "Are they napping?"

"They should be up any minute. You came home just at the right time."

The ding of the oven timer took her attention. Finally, the beef bourguignon was ready to come out of the oven. She drained the stew into a colander and then added it to the pot, stirring the onions and mushrooms in along with the sauce. It looked heavenly.

The first *waah* came a minute later.

She watched Theo head up the stairs and heard him making monster noises and blowing raspberries and then lots of baby laughter.

She smiled as she transferred the beef bourguignon and the garlic mashed potatoes into warming dishes, packed up the French bread, the green salad—Virginia was particular about dressing and liked to make her own, which she was known for—and dessert, a berry tart.

Theo came down with Ethan and Olivia in each arm, and she gave each tot a kiss on the head. "I'll go plop these guys in the playpen in the family room and then go get the others. Back in a flash." Two minutes later, he was back with Tyler and Henry, who also got a kiss each from her, then he disappeared into the family room.

She could hear them all playing and squealing. She'd join them for a minute, but between being exhausted from working on this masterpiece of a stew for the past five hours and now having to deliver it and deal with Virginia, who could be…strident, Allie let Theo know she'd be back in twenty minutes and headed out.

As she drove to Virginia's Colonial, she realized she'd be passing right by the new house. She pulled up in front and stared at it, and once again, just the sight of it, its specialness, its magical rightness, the pretty Christmas lights, filled her with hope. In less than two weeks, she would be moving here. With her husband and children, starting a new life.

But as she realized she'd better get a move on it and

pulled away from the curb, she had a terrible, horrible, awful thought.

That Theo might have bought the house for them because it *was* so big and roomy and he could keep himself at a distance there the way he couldn't in their tiny Victorian. Maybe he figured that if she was going to marry Elliot Talley to give her children a father and security, then she'd be happy having their actual father doing the same, that it didn't matter if their relationship worked or not. They could lead separate lives—together.

She shook her head. No. That wasn't why he'd bought the house. He was just getting used to his new life, being a family man.

As her sister had said, everything would be okay.

It was all she wanted for Christmas, so it had better be okay.

As Allie pulled into Virginia's driveway at precisely the time she was told to arrive, a good half hour before her sister-in-law was due, she told herself to stop thinking about Theo and start thinking about getting everything set up in Virginia's kitchen to look as though her client had made everything herself. She'd offered to cook right in Virginia's kitchen, but Virginia was in a mood and just wanted Allie to make it look that way when she arrived.

Allie grabbed her heavy bags and brought them inside, then spent ten minutes making a faux scene of a woman who'd been cooking for hours but was Virginia Gelman, so still had a practically spotless kitchen. The warming stew would fill the kitchen with its breathtaking aroma and no one would be the wiser.

Allie Stark, ghostcook. Allie Stark, ghostwife.

She shivered, not liking either.

As she was leaving, out the back door, of course, Virginia asked how things were going with "that handsome husband," and Allie said pretty well, they were getting used to each other again. *Talking too much, as usual, Allie.* A "How are you?" was usually a throwaway comment that no one wanted a real answer to. Particularly Virginia Gelman.

"Want to know a secret?" Virginia asked, her expression quite serious all of a sudden.

Allie tilted her head. Did she?

"Tell no one. Do I have your word? Only two people know about this and they're both long gone, but every time I see you, Allie, I want to tell you. I'm not sure why, but I do."

Yeesh, what was this about? "You have my word, Virginia."

"I know I'm lauded at having been married for almost fifty-five years. But I was engaged once before to a real daredevil type. My parents hated him!"

Huh. "Is that why you didn't marry him?" she asked.

"Are you kidding? I would have run off with him and sat on the back of his motorcycle."

Allie smiled. She tried to imagine Virginia on the back of a motorcycle, her hair whipping in the wind, her arms wrapped around a daredevil in a leather jacket.

"He left me," she said, her expression so wistful that Allie stayed quiet to give her some privacy with her thoughts. "He wrote me a letter that said he knew I was a good girl and could never defy my parents and I'd be miserable with him and he loved me too much to make me miserable. So he left. I never saw him again."

Allie sucked in a breath. "Do you still think about him?"

"Of course. I always wonder what if. I love Edward and we've had a great marriage and I hope we will have many more years together. But my beau was who he was and I guess it's true I wouldn't have been able to accept it past a certain point. I'd want Sunday dinners with my parents. Children."

"Did he want children?" Allie asked.

"Motorcycle buckets full of them." She smiled and shook her head. "He wanted to name our firstborn Spike."

Allie laughed. "Spike. I love it."

"My list was a bit more classic," she said. "But hey, Spike could work as a nickname. My parents would have fainted, of course. If I could go back in time—" She stopped and shook her head. "Well, that's silly because I can't."

"But I want to know," Allie said. "If you could go back in time..."

"I would have stopped him from leaving. I would have said, let's try. Let's find middle ground. If you love me, you'll compromise. If I love you, I'll compromise. All marriage is about compromise. Even between the very compatible like me and Edward."

"And daredevils and good girls," Allie said.

"And moms of quadruplets and cops who take the most dangerous assignments," Virginia added.

"What if the middle ground is that both of us compromise to the point that we're making ourselves miserable?"

"If you want your marriage to Theo to work, just ask yourself—do we want to split up or do we want to do everything we can to save this marriage? I wish TJ had had more faith in me. Turns out I had it in myself."

Virginia lifted her chin as if trying to get control of her emotions, which probably wanted to tumble out of her. Allie wished she had more time before her sister-in-law got here. She wished she could be the one having dinner with Virginia and listen to her talk for hours.

"Do you think wanting to save the marriage is enough?" Allie asked. "If Theo distances himself emotionally to protect us both, what can I do?"

"You'll figure that out as you go along, Allie, as I'm sure you're doing. When to back off, when to steamroll. If you know your husband, you'll know when to do which."

"I'll do what I have to for you *and* me," Allie said with a smile, tears misting her eyes.

Virginia wrapped her in a hug. Just then the doorbell rang.

"Oh, no! We've been talking so long your guests are here! I'll leave my stuff, since it'll help look like you made everything, and come pick it up later." She hurried toward the sliding glass doors at the back of the house.

But Virginia caught her by the hand and frowned, then led her to the front door. She opened the door and there was a woman and man about Virginia's age, very well dressed.

"Joanne and Steven, so nice to see you. And you're so lucky that you get to meet chef Allie Stark. She cooked dinner tonight, soup to nuts."

"I thought I was having your fabulous beef bourguignon," Joanne said, lifting her nose in the air. "We were so looking forward."

"Joanne, I haven't made beef bourguignon once in my life. Allie has been cooking for me for years."

The woman's mouth dropped open. "Really? My God, all this time I thought I had to compete against Mrs. Perfection. I wish you'd told me years ago. What a relief that would have been."

The surprise in Virginia's eyes lit up her entire face. "Well, to new beginnings."

The previously snooty sister-in-law threw her arms around Virginia for a hug. "To new beginnings."

Huh. Honesty had won the day.

"Well, this is a nice development," the husband said, giving his brother, Virginia's husband, a hug.

Allie smiled. "Enjoy dinner," she said.

"Maybe we could have lunch, just us two," Virginia said.

"I'd like that," she said, giving Virginia's hand a squeeze.

She left, barely able to feel her feet. If Virginia Gelman could surprise her, anything was possible.

Good news when it came to Allie's life.

Back at home, Allie spent the evening coming up with new recipes for her gluten-free clients and thinking about Virginia's secret. It was crazy how you never knew what was going on with other people. All this time she thought Virginia Gelman was a snoot who cut corners and who'd never experienced real emotion. What the hell did Allie know about Virginia or her life? *Judge not*, as her mother used to say with a wag of her finger.

For the first time since Theo had returned to her life, she found herself thinking more of what he'd gone through than what she had. Yes, she'd been told her husband was dead—and when she was just seven weeks pregnant. She'd gone to his funeral. She'd sobbed in her bedroom for hours at a time at night. She'd given birth with her sisters by her side, thank God, wishing her late husband could see these four beautiful little beings they'd created and brought in the world. She'd had months to mourn Theo before they'd been born, but when she'd brought the quads home to this house, knowing they'd never know their father, she'd fallen into despair all over again. Luckily, four infants had a way of keeping a new mother very busy on all levels, and she'd focused on them.

But she'd never really stopped to think about Theo the night of the explosion. The panic at hearing that monster rattle off her name, her sisters' names, his father's room number at the nursing home. He'd given up so much—his loss made only slightly bearable, perhaps, because he thought disappearing from her life, forever, was the right thing for her, for her happiness. And for almost two years, he'd been living like a ghost on a remote cattle ranch in southern Wyoming, completely cut off from anything he'd known and been. He'd done that for her, for her family, for his father.

He hadn't been relieved to walk away. She knew that now. It had broken his heart that he thought he should in the first place. That she'd be better off.

Oh, Theo. She could hear him in the nursery, making up words to Brahms's *Lullaby*, using all their names and places in Wedlock Creek. She smiled and then almost cried.

I love you so much, Theo.

And a few minutes later, when he came into the bedroom, in his sexy army sweats and a T-shirt that showed off his incredible shoulders and arms, and slipped into bed beside her, she turned to face him.

"Talking is the key," she said. "No matter what, we have to talk. If something's bothering us, if something is wrong outside the marriage, in the marriage, we have to talk to each other. Deal?"

He held her gaze for a moment, as if thinking, *What brought this on?* But then he thought better of it, apparently. "Deal," he said. "It might take me a day or two, though. I'm used to keeping things bottled up."

"I know. But just try to tell me sooner than usual. Before it gets clogged in there," she said, patting his chest. His rock-hard chest.

She couldn't move her hand. Could not. Would not. Seriously, he'd have to make her.

And suddenly he was kissing her, passionately, his hands in her hair, roaming her back, pulling her closer.

"I've been dying to do this since…the last time," he said. "But…" He held her face between his hands and looked at her, his green eyes so intense on her.

"Forget the buts. We just have to communicate, Theo. So if you feel like running for the hills after, say so. And I'll go make you a great omelet and one of those berry smoothies you love, and we'll watch a movie, something funny, and we'll get through it. We just have to get through it, deal with what comes our way."

"Same goes for you," he said. "Say what you need to. I can take it."

"I know you can. But can you take this," she said, moving her hand lower under the blanket until he shuddered.

"No," he moaned. "I can't." He smiled and took her hands and held them over her head on the bed as he lay fully on top her, kissing everywhere he could reach.

And then she couldn't think anymore; she could only feel.

Chapter Twelve

In the morning, when Theo heard a baby cry, he wasn't imagining it or wishing it as a means to escape the bed and Allie's arm, which was flung over his shoulder. He really did hear a cry—and because he could differentiate between the quads now, he knew it was Tyler.

Fifteen-second rule, he reminded himself, this time not wanting to get out of this bed, to leave Allie's warm, sexy body for a minute. They'd made love twice last night. After the first time, they'd gone downstairs and she had made the talked-about Western omelet while he made the smoothies. They'd watched a Marvel movie and he'd had to tell her every superhero's backstory, but she'd liked the film, and then they'd checked on the babies, hand in hand, crib by crib, and he'd never felt closer to her ever. With the quads fast asleep, he'd picked her up and carried her into their bedroom, Allie kissing him en route, and they'd had amazing sex again.

Now, one ear peeled for another cry from Tyler and his eyes on his beautiful wife, he moved a strand of hair from her cheek and just drank in the sight of her. An award-show montage of moments of their lives popped into his head—seeing her trying to climb that tree to get the I'm-not-coming-down old cat, their first date at Mexicano Mike's, then her favorite restaurant, standing in the Wedlock Creek Wedding Chapel and watching his bride walk down the aisle toward him in that amazing white gown. A few not-so-happy moments tried to muscle their way into the montage, but Theo pushed them out of his mind. That was then, before. He was a different person now. And together, he and Allie were a new Mr. and Mrs. Stark.

"WAAAH!"

"That boy has some set of lungs," Allie said, snuggling closer against him and kissing him on the cheek. "I'll go."

"No, you sleep, I'll go. I need to get up and have ten cups of coffee, anyway. Difficult phone call to make this morning."

She glanced at him. "About the case?"

He nodded. "I'm hoping to meet with the barely four-foot-tall suspect's mother this morning." He gave Allie another kiss and was about to tell her how great last night was, but Tyler screeched again, followed by Olivia. Then all four babies joined in on the concert.

"The neighbors will be thrilled when we move," Allie said, slipping her feet into the fuzzy dog slippers one of her sisters had given her.

"Hey, you live in Wedlock Creek, land of the multiples, you gotta expect lots of simultaneous crying at all hours."

She laughed and they headed into the nursery, Allie lifting up the black-out shades, flooding the room with sunshine.

They took care of the babies, got them downstairs and took their turn to shower. All ate breakfast, and then Theo finally excused himself back upstairs to make that call to Hunter Chadwell's mother. School vacation started today and Christmas was in just five days. He hated adding to Mrs. Chadwell's grief, particularly at such a difficult time of year to be in mourning. But it was a call he had to make.

He closed the bedroom door and sat at the desk, pressing in the Chadwell number on his cell phone. June Chadwell answered and he introduced himself.

"Is it about the Christmas presents going missing around the neighborhood?" she asked. "We haven't been targeted, thank heavens. I only have two gifts for my son, and I'd be devastated if one was stolen."

Theo's heart squeezed. "Well, it's about that, but I'll explain in person." He set up a meeting for nine, not looking forward to this visit at all, though it always felt good to wrap up a case.

He went back down to the kitchen to find Allie on the phone, and from the sounds of it, she was being hired to cater a party.

"Huh. Virginia Gelman's sister-in-law not only hired me to cater her New Year's party, but three calls have come in at her recommendation for standing gigs for meal deliveries."

"Wow," he said. "I guess the beef bourguignon was a big hit."

"Oh, it was," she said, a cryptic smile on her beautiful face.

"So I'm meeting with the potential suspect's mother at nine," he said. "You're okay on your own for a good hour?"

"Absolutely. Merry's school vacation started today, so she's coming over in a little while to see her nephews and niece."

He nodded, gave each quad a kiss and then left. Time to deal with a tiny thief.

A For Sale sign was posted in the front yard of 112 Oak Hill Road. Theo thought back to what Merry had said about June Chadwell's financial situation. So much loss. A husband and father. A home. Theo wasn't one to excuse bad behavior, particularly criminal behavior, but in certain circumstances he liked to understand motivation. A seven-year-old was going around his neighborhood stealing his classmates' Christmas presents. The motive wasn't hard to speculate on. Hunter *wanted*, plain and simple. And he was taking.

He rang the bell. June Chadwell, midthirties, her brown hair in a ponytail, opened the door. She looked tired. And world-weary. He followed her to the living room, where she gestured for him to sit. As he took the love seat facing the chair Mrs. Chadwell sat on, he noticed a little boy playing outside in the fenced yard with a small dog, throwing a ball that the dog would fetch.

He explained the situation to Mrs. Chadwell, the missing presents, the visit to Ms. Finley, and as June's shoulders slumped he knew the exact moment she realized why he was there.

"I want to be able to say that my Hunter wouldn't have done such a thing, that he couldn't have stolen those gifts," Mrs. Chadwell said. "But these days, everything is so upside down with both of us that anything is poss—" She burst into tears.

Theo grabbed the box of tissues on the coffee table and moved to the chair next to her and handed her the box. "This has to be a very tough time, Mrs. Chadwell. Especially now, three months after you lost your husband."

"What do you mean?" she asked.

"I don't claim to know how you feel because I've never been in your shoes," he said. "But I remember my wife telling me that around three months after she got the news that I'd been killed, she felt most alone. The calls and visits and meal trains had stopped. She wasn't invited to get-togethers or parties because the hosts either felt uncomfortable or didn't want to invite a single person instead of a couple. I could go on. But it was the time she felt most isolated and alone when she needed people desperately."

June Chadwell dabbed under her eyes with a tissue. "That's exactly how I feel. Exactly. I couldn't even really put it into thoughts or words."

He nodded. "Very understandable. Because your life is topsy-turvy," he said. "And sometimes, we think kids are okay because they're playing or laughing or excited about getting a new toy, and we fall back on how resilient they are when they're actually hurting just as badly as we are."

She glanced out the sliding glass doors, where Hunter

Chadwell, a slip of a kid in jeans and a blue down jacket, hat and mittens, was throwing the ball. Theo could hear him shouting, "Get it, Snickers, get it! Good Snickers!"

"Perhaps you could check his room, his closet, to see if the gifts are hidden there? I want to make clear that I don't know that Hunter is the thief. It's just a possibility."

She nodded. "Why don't you come with me? His room is just across the hall."

Hunter followed her to the boy's bedroom, posters from Star Wars and the Harry Potter movies on the walls. She went over to the closet and opened it, then kneeled down. A gray blanket was spread out in the back, covering a heap of…something.

"Oh, no," she said, shaking her head. She pulled away the blanket and there were a stack of wrapped gifts. She lifted one of the name tags. "For Miles."

Theo nodded. He checked the other name tags—all for kids whose gifts had been stolen. "Let's leave these here for the time being and go talk to Hunter."

She took a deep breath and they went back into the living room. She slid open the glass door and called in her son.

Hunter came running in, Snickers on his trail. The dog gave Theo a sniff, then went to his water bowl and lapped up a drink, then hopped on the sofa.

"Hunter, sweetie, this is Sergeant Theo Stark. He's a police officer."

Hunter's eyes widened and his face crumpled. He began sobbing, tears running down his cheeks. Snickers stood up on the sofa and jumped off, then ran over to the boy and stood beside him. The boy dropped to his knees and wrapped his arms around the dog.

"Am I going to jail?" he asked, slashing a forearm under his eyes. The tears kept falling.

"No," Theo said, kneeling down in front of him. "I promise you that you don't have to worry about that." He smiled at the kid. "Do you know why I'm here?"

"'Cause you found out I took presents?" the boy said through a fresh round of sobs.

Theo nodded. "That's right. Can you tell your mom and me why you took the presents? You knew they didn't belong to you, right?"

"I know. I went to kids' houses from my class when I knew they wouldn't be there. And I took one of the presents for them."

"Why, Hunter?" his mom asked, her voice clogged with emotion.

He shrugged his scrawny shoulders. "I just wanted them."

His mom took his hand and rubbed his back. "Hunter, you know that stealing is wrong."

Hunter wiped under his eyes. "I know. I was just so mad about a lot of stuff." His face crumpled again. "Like about Daddy and moving and that I couldn't go to karate and they got to."

"They being the boys in your class?" Theo asked.

Hunter nodded.

"Why don't you take Snickers back outside for a minute. I'll talk to your mom and then we'll call you back in when we're ready, okay?"

The boy looked relieved to get away. His mother closed the glass door behind him, then sat across from Theo again.

"What now?" she said. "How should this be handled?"

"Well, in large part it's been handled—he was caught, a policeman came to his house to talk to his mother and to him. That goes a long way with a seven-year-old. I think I'd like to call the parents involved and talk to them, then have Hunter return each gift to each tree and apologize to the families. All the gifts are accounted for and he didn't even open any, which is a good sign. That he knew he shouldn't."

She nodded. "Thank you, Sergeant Stark."

"Any offers on the house?" he asked.

"Actually, I heard from the real estate agent this morning that we have an offer. I'd like to move before the new year so that I can start Hunter at a new school when the winter break is over. I think a fresh start would do us both good. Especially after all this."

"Agreed," he said. "And looks like he'll have a good buddy coming with him."

They both turned and watched Hunter sitting very quietly on the deck steps, his head on his folded arms on his knees, the dog sitting beside him.

"I'll be in touch about setting up the return of the gifts. I'd like to do it quickly and have him able to return the presents in a short period of time."

She nodded again, and he stood up.

"If you ever need anything, Mrs. Chadwell, I want you to give me a call, okay?" he said. "Help finding a job or if Hunter needs someone to talk to. Okay?"

Tears misted her eyes and she nodded. "Thank you so much. And Merry Christmas."

"Merry Christmas."

* * *

Theo sat in his truck outside Hunter's home, giving himself a moment to decompress. But he didn't. Or couldn't. A weight had settled over his shoulders. He couldn't stop thinking about how Tyler, Henry, Ethan and Olivia had almost been consigned to a life without their dad—before they were even born. At two, three, asking where their dad was, Allie having to tell them he was in heaven, and meanwhile, he would be none the wiser on a cattle ranch seven hours away.

It's pointless to even think about this, he knew. *Moot. The past.* But still, the thoughts clung.

And of course, the situations were hardly the same. Hunter was a seven-year-old who'd had his dad his whole life until three months ago. The boy was in the throes of grief. Theo's children never would have known him. They'd have been raised with a kindly father figure. Not that that had gone according to plan with Elliot Talley.

Thank God. The thought of Allie with anyone else, married to another guy, another man raising his beloved quadruplets sent acid coursing through his gut. And a rush of sadness. How could he have ever believed Allie would have been better off without him? That was a coward's move, a coward's way of thinking.

Or just the thinking of someone without hope, without choice.

Now he had all the hope in the world. But come January, when he went back to work, he'd risk his life on a daily basis. Those were the cases he'd be assigned, what he was trained for: the most dire of circumstances.

Every day he'd kiss the quads goodbye, kiss his wife

goodbye, and maybe he wouldn't come back one night. Except this time around, he'd really be dead. He tried to shake these inane thoughts that made no sense. Of course, his job came with risk.

And now he'd put his family at risk of losing him. Of Tyler, Henry, Ethan and Olivia five, seven, nine, however many years old, having Mommy tell them that Daddy had been killed in the line of duty. Those four precious faces crumpling, their hearts breaking, their faith in the world shaken.

He shuddered in his seat.

So what was he thinking? That the four Stark babies were better off not having him in their lives at all so that they wouldn't know the pain of losing the father they loved so much? That made no sense.

Right?

More heavyhearted than he'd been five minutes ago, Theo started up the truck and drove away, no idea where he was going. But not home.

Chapter Thirteen

Allie was just about ready to deliver to Angela Sattler a week's worth of reheatable Weight Watchers–friendly dinners, all based on the number of "points" she was allowed to have per day. Angela had given Allie a list of her favorite meals—spaghetti carbonara, meat loaf with garlic mashed potatoes and onion soup with cheese and croutons. Not the easiest three dishes to re-create healthy low-cal, low-fat versions of, but Allie had managed. The carbonara had come out particularly good, if Allie did say so herself.

"Sure you're okay on your own?" her sister Merry asked as she put on her down jacket. Her sister had come to watch the quads while Allie focused on her work in the kitchen. Theo had texted that he'd be home at two thirty, which was perfect, since she had to have the meals delivered to Angela's at three.

"Yup," Allie said, glancing at her sister. "What are you going to wear tonight?" Merry had a hot date with a journalist at the *Wedlock Creek Gazette*. "Don't forget to pick that Cheerio out of your hair," Allie added, gesturing at the ends of Merry's strawberry blond curls.

"I just might leave it there," Merry said. "This isn't a *real* date. He's the divorced father of triplet girls and wants the secrets I, as one of triplets, can share."

Allie laughed. "He told you that?"

"Yes, actually."

"Huh. You might like this guy. He sounds like your type."

"The type who says it like it is. A straight shooter. We'll see." She picked up Olivia from her high chair and gave her a kiss. Olivia babbled and pulled down one of Merry's springy curls, sending the Cheerio to the floor.

Merry laughed. "Well, now I'm ready for my date. Thanks, O."

She gave Olivia's three brothers a kiss goodbye and then left.

Allie wondered if Merry would ever settle down. But in the next moment, Henry let out a screech, so all thoughts about her sister's love life went *poof* from her head.

She glanced at the clock. Theo had texted her an hour ago to let her know he'd be home around two thirty. Well, it was two forty-five and no sign of him.

That was one long meeting with the little suspect's mother. Clearly he'd been somewhere between then and now, but when she texted, How'd the meeting go? he texted back a terse Tell you later.

When the clock chimed three o'clock, Allie sighed, stared at her warming bag of packed meals and said, "Well, kids, guess you're coming with me. Just like old times."

One by one she got the quads in their jackets, then two by two into their car seats in the SUV. Then she grabbed her bags of meals from the kitchen table and then finally got herself in the car with an *Okay, we're on our way.* Of course, halfway down the road, she realized she'd forgotten her purse and had to drive back to the house. *Do I have my head?* she seriously wondered, reaching up to make sure it was attached to her shoulders. *Yes. There it is.*

By the time she delivered Angela's meals and got the quads back home, Theo's truck still wasn't in the driveway. Fear raced up her spine, and then she narrowed her eyes and crossed her arms over her chest. *Is this how it's gonna be? Him disappearing all day, barely a text, and then me scared spitless that he's either hurt somewhere or has run for the hills?*

No. That was *not* how it was going to be. She would not live her life that way. Last night he'd promised—okay, *agreed*—that they'd talk if there was a problem, he'd say what was on his mind, what was bothering him. He wasn't "allowed" to distance himself. That was the old Theo.

Maybe it's not even about you, she told herself, springing Olivia from her car seat and placing her in the giant stroller. Henry was next. "In you go," she told him, giving him a kiss on his head. Maybe he had a terrible morning with the boy who'd stolen the presents, the mother had freaked out, punched him, and he had to arrest her. Who the hell knew? Anything could happen when you were married to a cop.

About to put Tyler in the stroller, she bit her lip and glanced up and down the street for Theo's black pickup. No sign of it.

Where was he?

And was he coming back?

After leaving the Chadwells, Theo had gone to the police station and filled in his captain, then called the four homes that had been targeted by Hunter and spoken with three moms and one dad, explaining about Hunter and the plan to return the gifts and apologize. All four parents had been surprised, as Theo had been, that Hunter hadn't opened any of the gifts. Three had added an "aww." The dad was the lone holdout but had said, "Poor kid. Has to be going through a really rough time."

And so tomorrow, at 2:00 pm, he'd pick up Hunter and his mom and the gifts, and he'd accompany Hunter on the return and apology tour.

With all that settled, he found himself driving around, not ready to head home, not interested in going anywhere. He needed something and he had no damned idea what it was.

His phone pinged with a text. Oh, no—Allie. He'd told her he'd back by two thirty and then had gotten so caught up in his head that he'd driven around and lost track of time. He'd forgotten to text her back.

I'm sorry. Big day. On my way home.

Good, she texted back.

For some reason, that made him smile, even if it meant he was in trouble.

He was going home.

He started up the engine, but his phone rang, so he turned the engine back off. He figured it was Allie and he couldn't wait to hear her voice. He hoped she wasn't too pissed at him. She had every right to be. But he had a lot to tell her.

He grabbed his phone. It wasn't Allie. It was the captain.

He listened to the captain talk, his heart starting to pound, every cell in his body alert.

"I'll need your answer by noon tomorrow, Stark," the captain said, then signed off.

He sat in the pickup for a good fifteen minutes, thinking about all the captain had told him. Thinking about Allie. The past. The present. The future, which he wasn't too sure about.

Everything was riding on his response.

He had no idea what the hell to do.

Ever since Theo had gotten home last night, he'd been quiet. Contemplative, Allie had realized, and had decided to let him be. She made him a cup of chamomile tea, light and sweet the way he liked the herbal stuff, and when it was gone, she made him another, adding a toasted bagel and vegetable cream cheese, since he hadn't eaten much at dinner, let alone said much.

All she knew was that he'd squared away the present-thief case and would finish up with that tomorrow, then had driven around to clear his head.

Somewhere in all that was the key to why he was so distant. And though they'd agreed to talk, to not do exactly what they were doing, which was for one to not talk while the other fretted and speculated, Allie let him do what he needed. Something was up, or bothering him, and he'd talk when he was ready.

In the morning, he was playful with the quads, crawling around the family room with them, singing the alphabet song, but he was still quiet, still inside his own head.

When the babies were finally all down for their naps and the two left the nursery, Theo gave her a tight smile.

"I'd better get going. Reed's multiples seminar starts at eleven thirty. And then I'll be picking up Hunter and his mom at two," he said. "Long day," he added. For a moment she thought he was about to say something else, but he didn't.

"Before you go, I need to know something," she said.

He put a hand on the post of the stair railing as if to brace himself. "Okay."

"What's going on, Theo? And don't say it's nothing because something clearly is. We'd said we'd talk to each other."

"Let's go into the kitchen," he said, his expression somewhere between somber and conflicted.

Well, at least she was right about her Theo-radar. He had something big on his mind.

In the kitchen, he gestured at the table, and she sat down, which made her even more on red alert, since this was a "you'd better sit down" type of thing.

"Coffee?" he asked, taking out her favorite mug even though she hadn't answered.

"Sure," she said. If the man needed to "do" something in order to say what he had to say, fine.

He poured the coffee and added sugar and cream the way she liked, then handed her the mug. "Captain Morgan wants me on the force tomorrow. For a new task force the local FBI field office is spearheading."

Allie almost dropped the mug. She set it on the table, mentally shaking her head at what he'd said. Christmas was in just a few days. They should be doing their holiday shopping at the very crowded mall or window-shopping in county seat Brewster's vibrant downtown. Not having this conversation—that would mean no Christmas at all. Not one with Theo there.

"To cut to the chase," he said quickly, "it's about organized crime. One particular thug the PD and local FBI have been after for six months has resurfaced. The captain asked for my help."

Allie tried to keep her expression neutral, but inside she was shouting, *Noooooo!* She picked up the mug and took a swig of her coffee, the caffeine boost helpful.

She stared at him, this man she'd known for so long, and she could see that he wanted to be part of this task force, that were it not for her and the quads, he'd be at the PD now.

"I'd have to be away for days at a time, possibly, while working surveillance," he said. "We can't know the extent until we're in it, really."

I love you. And if I love you, I have to let you be who you are. But I have to protect myself. She took another sip of the coffee, an idea forming in her head that she wasn't sure of.

"I know you want to join the task force. I know this is the kind of police work you feel you're meant to do, Theo. I don't want to take that from you."

He stared at her. "Not the reaction I expected."

"But," she added.

"But," he prompted.

"But I can't go back to two years ago. Things are good between us, Theo. We have a beautiful family life. I want to protect that. But I also need to protect myself."

"What are you saying?" he asked.

"That maybe there's a way we can make this work. You can do the work you want and I—and our marriage—won't be in the same vulnerable position as I was back then."

He poured himself a cup of coffee and sat down. "I've been racking my brain all night, Allie. I've come up with nothing. So I'm more than a little wary of whatever you're going to say."

She could barely get the words out—that was how wary she was of the idea in the first place. But what choice did they have?

"Theo, I was about to marry Elliot Talley for the sake of the children. So they could have a father, stability and security. The marriage would have been basically platonic, since there was very little romance between him and me. I suppose he had his reason for proposing and for dropping out. And now you and I have ours."

"Ours?" he asked, looking at her as though he was not following. And frankly, who would be following this crazy train of thought?

"A reason for having a marriage based on something other than romance. We'd live like partners and roommates," she said. "Raising our children. But otherwise we'd live separate lives. I wouldn't expect the usual stuff a wife expects from her husband, and therefore, there would be no stomped-on expectations or hopes."

"Like roommates," he repeated, his voice almost cracking.

"Right. You're not here for me or this marriage. You're here for the kids. So let's make it about them."

That wasn't entirely fair. She knew he loved her. She did believe that. But she also believed that Theo Stark had romanticized his homecoming, thought they could pick up where they left off—minus all the heartache—and start anew, only to realize they would soon be back in the same situation they'd been in two years ago. The "but," the monkey wrench, came in the form of the four babies upstairs. Theo had become a father the day he returned and that changed everything. But not between *them*.

He stared at her. "Allie, this isn't what I want. And it can't be what you want."

"What I want is for you to be happy, Theo. I want you to be the cop you want to be, who you need to be. If that's chasing mobsters and getting shot at, well, that's what you signed up for. I didn't realize, I guess, that it's what I signed up for when I married a small-town police officer. I thought your biggest cases would be expired registrations and arguments over cutting in line at the bagel shop on Saturday mornings or maybe the occasional burglary. I thought you'd be chasing down seven-year-old present thieves, Theo."

He took another swig of his coffee and then leaned his head back. “I know.”

“Now I have four kids to think about. They come first for me. So I want to stay with their father. But I have to change everything about how I view our marriage. We’d be parenting partners.”

“Parenting partners? That doesn’t sound right, either, Allie. Platonic spouses?”

Stay strong, she told herself. “I can’t say goodbye to you in the morning when you’re on this task force and not know if you’ll come home, if you’ll need to fake your own death again because you witnessed the mobster do something awful. I need to keep boundaries.”

“This isn’t what I want, Allie.”

“It’s not what I want, either. But it’s a solution.”

He shook his head.

She glanced at the clock on the wall. “The multiples seminar starts in fifteen minutes. You’d better get going.”

“This conversation isn’t over,” he said.

What was left to say?

“I love you, Allie,” he said, standing up. “We’ll figure it out.”

She already had.

Chapter Fourteen

Parenting partners.

Platonic spouses.

Theo shook his head as he took the stairs up to the second floor of the Wedlock Creek Community Center and headed for Room 209. There was no way in hell Allie's idea could work. He couldn't live that way. He didn't *want* to live that way. And he knew she didn't, either.

You're not exactly giving her much choice, he reminded himself.

As he pulled open the door to the room where Reed Barelli's two-hour seminar, "New Dads of Multiples," was being held, he breathed a sigh of relief. He counted twelve men sitting at desks, notebooks at the ready. He wasn't the only one in desperate need of this class. Reed's wife, Norah, taught many of the multiples classes, but when she'd brought Reed in for a "father's perspective" one time, the class had been such a hit that Reed began offering a seminar for new dads twice a semester.

Juggling multiples, a job, life—and teaching classes? Reed had this down. And Theo needed this class bigtime.

The timing couldn't be better. Theo would get some great tips, more in depth than what Reed had been able to share in the busy, loud Kidz Zone with both their attention on their children. Now Theo could soak up solid information and have a much better chance of talking Allie out of this platonic marriage nightmare. Because that was what it would be: a nightmare. If he could just show her—and himself—that it was possible to be a family man and a cop who worked mostly in the most dangerous of shadows and circumstances, then they could still have what they'd been working toward: their family.

Allie and him, platonic? He wouldn't survive a night. He'd barely survived those first few nights at her side in their bed.

"Welcome!" Reed said from the front of the room. "You know, when I first started teaching this seminar, I used to have a five-page handout for every student. If you look at the desk in front of me, you'll see I don't have any handouts. Know why? Because when your twins or triplets or quadruplets are screaming their heads off all at the same time, you're not going to be consulting the manual."

Theo laughed. He tried to imagine himself looking up "How to change four diapers at once" while the quads cried and lifted their arms.

"The most important things you need to know about being the father or caretaker of multiples?" Reed posed to a group hanging on his every word. "Number one—you're doing better than you think you are. Even if one triplet is screeching bloody murder and another is breaking out in hives and the third is taking off his diaper and throwing it across the room—you're doing better than you think. Because you're trying. And you'll soon come into a rhythm. At first, everything will seem overwhelming and then one day you'll realize you've got this, that you're handling it, that you can tell Billy and Brandon apart."

Theo knew from experience all that was true. He thought back to the first day he'd met Tyler, Henry, Ethan and Olivia, how inept he'd felt. Now he could change one's diaper while sprinkling cornstarch on another's tush without blinking. He'd learned how to feed four babies at once. And he could tell which baby was crying in the middle of night at first *waah*.

Reed continued on about using safe stations—high chairs, Exersaucers, playpens, car seats, cribs—to contain a baby or two if it were necessary to concentrate on another. After a talk on safety in general, he moved to schedules—feeding, napping, sleeping, diaper changes, playtime.

"Okay, pop quiz on material we haven't even covered yet," Reed said. "It's eight thirty. You have to be at work at nine. You still have to get dressed and have some coffee. Your wife is on maternity leave and both twins are crying. What do you do?"

A guy in a suit raised his hand. "You let your wife handle it."

"Sorry, my friend, but that is incorrect," Reed said. "Just because your wife is on leave and you're not doesn't mean the babies are her sole responsibility. You're there, you help. You take one baby, she takes one baby. In no time, the situation is handled. And guess what? It took two minutes. Now your wife is smiling and feels supported, and you got to spend more quality time with your family."

There were murmurs and nods. "Never looked at it that way," another guy said. "But I get it."

"Quiz question number two. It's seven o'clock at night. Your wife expected you home an hour ago. You have six-month-old quadruplets. Your boss gives you a plum assignment that will work in your favor come promotion time, but he wants you to stay late every day for the next two weeks to handle it. What do you do?"

"Work has to come first," Andrew Muttler, a mortgage broker, said.

"Agreed," said a lawyer.

Theo raised up a hand. "Well, I don't agree that work has to come first, but I don't know what the answer is."

And he needed the answer.

"The answer is compromise," Reed said. "You want the big assignment? Fine. Tell your boss you can only take it on if you can do the extra work it'll require from home."

"Huh," the lawyer said. "I guess I can do most what I do via Wi-Fi and my briefcase."

Reed nodded. "Exactly."

"But what if I'm deep in concentration at 9:00 p.m.

on the project at home, and the babies start crying and I can't be interrupted?"

"Then you ask your wife if she can handle it this time," Theo said, "and you'll get it next time."

"Good compromise," Reed said, nodding at Theo.

But what about when I'm out on the street, behind some dark building, chasing down a suspect and a lead comes in, and if I go home, I lose the suspect. I can't take my work home with me. Literally and figuratively.

You'll figure it out, he told himself. Weren't those his last words to Allie earlier? He didn't have the same responsibilities two years ago. He didn't have four little lives depending on him. He had to change his way of thinking. He *would* figure it out.

Yeah? So how? There was no calling home or leaving early when you were on surveillance and had a suspect in your crosshairs. When getting the punk off the streets was the most important thing in that moment. *In that moment* seemed the key. Or was he just rationalizing?

Who was he kidding? He knew what was required to be a good cop in the field on these task forces. And he knew what was required of a father of baby quadruplets. Of a man who'd let his wife down hard once already and had vowed never to do it again.

He wanted to ask Barelli all these questions, but he was the only cop in the class and didn't want to take class time asking questions that only pertained to him. Reed had moved on to dealing with in-laws, and while Theo's mind focused on how he couldn't have it all, class had come to an end.

His heart so heavy he could barely stand up, Theo wondered if maybe Allie was right about the platonic marriage thing. He'd just have to give up his dreams of having a real marriage, of making love to Allie, of being partners in every sense of the word. He couldn't have everything, but he had to be there for her and the babies.

He glanced at his watch. Time to go pick up the Chadwells. And just as he was about to think, *Well, at least this assignment will let me take my mind off my problems with Allie*, he realized that *was* the problem. Getting consumed by his work and forgetting about what was tearing him apart inside.

What the hell was he going to do?

Hunter Chadwell sat in the back seat of Theo's car, staring down at his lap. His mother, June, sat in the passenger seat, biting her lip. He felt for her; no one wanted to be in her shoes, the mom of the kid who'd stolen his classmates' presents. And now had to face the music.

Theo pulled up in front of the Dumfords' residence. "Ready, Hunter?" Theo asked, turning around to look at the boy.

"I guess," he said, his face crumpling.

"Hey," Theo said. "You made a mistake and did something wrong. Now you're making it right. It feels good to make something right. Takes a huge weight off your shoulders. It's not going to be easy to walk into that house, Hunter, but after, you'll feel so much better."

The boy sniffled and nodded.

Moments later, the three of them stood on the doorstep of the Dumfords, Hunter holding the gift that belonged to Miles Dumford. Theo rang the bell.

Mrs. Dumford opened the door and smiled at him and Mrs. Chadwell, then looked at Hunter. "Hi there,

Hunter," she said, giving him a warm smile, which Theo appreciated. "Come on in."

The group followed her into the living room. The beautifully decorated tree was in front of the window, lined with presents underneath. Miles was sitting on the couch playing on an electronic device.

"Honey, look who's here," Mrs. Dumford said to her son. "It's Hunter."

The three of them stood somewhat awkwardly near the sofa. Theo nodded at Hunter, who held the wrapped gift in his hands and stepped closer to Miles.

"Um, Miles? I came into your house when you were at karate and took this. I'm really sorry." He handed it to Miles, then Miles's mom took it and put it on the coffee table.

"Why'd you take it?" Miles asked, tilting his head, his blond hair flopping to the side.

Hunter chewed on his lip and shrugged miserably, then said, "I was mad that you got to go to karate when I couldn't. I was riding my bike past your house and saw the Christmas tree, so I came in and looked for a present with your name and I took it."

"Why can't you go to karate?" Miles asked.

Theo could kiss the boy. Only kids got right to the heart of the matter, asking the right questions, leading right to motive. Adults tended to get sidetracked with all sorts of other issues.

"My mom said we couldn't pay for it," Hunter told him.

"Oh," Miles said. "Well, thanks for bringing it back. My mom told me it's the Lego set I wanted."

Hunter's eyes lit up for a moment at the words *Lego*

set, then he seemed to remember why he was here. "Sorry I took it."

"Maybe you can help me build it after I open it," Miles said.

His mother smiled. June Chadwell smiled. Theo smiled. And no one smiled bigger than Hunter.

"We might move right after Christmas," Hunter said. "But if we don't, I'll help you put it together. I'm good at Legos."

The next hour was a repeat, with minor tweaks here and there, of what had happened at the Dumfords'. Two of the kids weren't as willing to forgive and forget and invite Hunter to play with the item he'd stolen, but hey, no one said they had to. At the final house, the boy who had his ant farm taken was a total gem who was more interested in telling Hunter about ants and how they operated than anything else. The kid's little sister, who the present was from, walked up to Hunter and hugged him with a thank-you for returning the present. The mission ended on a good note.

"You were right, Policeman Stark," Hunter said to Theo as he helped him get settled into his car seat in the back of Theo's truck. "I feel better."

"Good," Theo said. "And we have a deal, right? No more stealing? If you feel bad about something and you're all upset inside, you'll talk to your teacher or your mom or you'll call me. You have the card I gave you, right?"

Hunter pulled it from his pocket and held it up, smiling. "I have it."

"Thank you so much," his mother whispered to

Theo as he got in the driver's seat. "For the first time in months, I feel like we're going to be okay."

He smiled and nodded and looked in the rearview mirror at Hunter, whose blue eyes had lost the troubled fear that had poked at Theo since he'd met him.

He imagined it was Tyler or Olivia in the back seat, having gotten in trouble.

He had to be there for them the way he'd been there for Hunter, the way he'd be there for Hunter. He couldn't be both. He couldn't be a family man and a cop who took on dangerous missions. Hadn't his own dad proved that? The man hadn't been there for Theo in the big ways.

Because he lost his wife, Theo's mother, because of his work. Theo didn't like to think about it and he never talked about it. He'd been young when his mother was killed, only four. He barely remembered the tall brunette with the kind green eyes and big smile. But he remembered his dad sitting him down and telling him his mother had been taken from them, that a bad man killed her and that Clinton Stark was going to make sure all the bad men in town were rounded up and sent to jail.

He'd thought his father was a hero. He still thought that. But his father had never been home, and Theo had been largely raised by his aunt. And as Theo grew up and listened to his dad's rants about everything from people to politics, he'd realized he disagreed with just about everything the man believed—except for ridding the streets of bad guys. It was their only common ground, and now that he thought about it, Theo had clung to it.

His father had done the best he could, Theo had told

himself over the years, not really sure if that was true or not. It had been his aunt's refrain and Theo hadn't liked it. *But his best isn't good enough*, Theo had always thought. Then felt small for feeling that way. Clinton Stark had missed many birthdays altogether, not even trying to get home before midnight, when Theo would be waiting up at nine, ten, eleven, for his father to burst into his room with a "Happy Birthday and I got the thug." His dad was just never around.

And the price? A relationship with his son. The rift between them had widened with every year, it seemed.

Almost like he wanted to protect me from him, he thought vaguely, then froze.

Wait a minute. Could that be the reason his father distanced himself even when Theo was as an adult? To protect Theo—to protect himself—from being close? Theo had never thought about it that way before, but maybe that was the case.

Hell, it probably was.

And that's what you're doing, he thought. *Protecting yourself from getting too close to Allie and the quads.* The new task force would make sure of that.

Go see Dad, he told himself. *Make your peace before it's too late. Because not everyone is lucky enough to get second chances.* And with his father he wouldn't.

He drove over to the nursing home and checked in at the desk. The receptionist called up to his dad's wing and let Theo know his father was having dinner in the floor café, which consisted of medically monitored meals.

He found Clinton Stark sitting at a table for two with his aide, a nice young woman named Delia, who had an easy smile. His heart constricted in his chest at the sight of his father, a napkin tucked inside his shirt, his gray hair still thick and brushed back like always.

"I'll let you join him," Delia said. "See you a little later, Mr. Stark," she added to his dad.

His dad glanced up at Theo. "Mr. Stark? Nice to meet you." He held out his hand and Theo shook it, but didn't let go. These types of lapses used to kill Theo, but he supposed he'd gotten used to it. His father not recalling the name Stark at all, or sometimes confusing Theo for his own father, and oftentimes assuming he worked at the home.

"Hi, Dad," he said. "I see you're having chicken soup with carrots. I remember you always liked that." His aunt had often made huge batches that were from his mom's recipe, and Theo had always felt close to her and happier when he was eating her chicken soup. His dad had a bowl every night. Theo hadn't really thought about what that really meant before now.

Clinton Stark hadn't been the easiest person to deal with, but Theo had always appreciated that his father had never tried to erase his mom's memory. Photographs of her remained up, no matter who he dated or how long the relationships lasted. And long after his aunt had stopped coming around as often, his father had made the soup every Sunday for as long as Theo had lived at home. His heart constricted at the thought of these little things—big things—that he'd missed because he'd been too focused on what he felt he'd been denied.

Make amends, he told himself. *Now is your chance.*

"I've missed you," Theo said, holding on to his dad's

left hand so he could eat with his right. "I've been a real idiot. About a lot of things."

His father glanced up at him, slowly bringing a spoonful of soup to his mouth. "Ah, this soup is darn good."

Theo smiled. "Like Mom used to make, right?"

"Mom? Mom's here?" Clinton looked around, his green eyes brightening, but the light dimmed and he shrugged, turning his attention back to his soup.

"You want to know what I think?" Theo whispered, his hand on his dad's shoulder. "I think we all do the best we can at the time. Whatever that might be in the moment. Might not be good enough for others and maybe it really isn't, but it's the best we can do at the time."

He thought back to all those times he'd felt wronged by his dad, the arguments about their viewpoints and politics and how Theo should live his life. His dad was his dad and he had to love him as he was if he wanted a father. Especially now when there wasn't much time left.

"I love you, Dad," he whispered. "I never thanked you for making Mom's chicken soup every Sunday. I never thanked you for keeping her photographs all over the house. You never talked about her, but you thought about her and now I know that. I always thought you were forcing your viewpoints on me, but it turns out you let me have my mom my way, my memories, young as I was. You let me remember her as I did."

He smiled, thinking about how he used to think Eliza Stark lived on a cloud high up in the sky. He'd told his dad that once when he was around six, and he'd never forget how Dad had said, *Yes, that's right.* Anything Theo had said about his mother, his dad's response had been *Yes, that's right.* No matter what. Theo had only had wonderful memories, so his dad's agreement had always been exactly what Theo had needed.

"You were a good father," Theo said, giving him a gentle hug.

Clinton looked at him, the light back, and Theo wondered if in that moment he knew who Theo was, heard what he said, felt the love radiating from his son. The light was gone seconds later, but Theo decided that in that brief, shining moment, his father had known.

Feeling better than he had in a long time, Theo accepted half of the dinner roll his dad offered him from the plate on the table, and sat there, just watching his father eat his soup and nod and smile at people getting up from other tables or sitting down.

When his father starting nodding off, Delia appeared and said she'd bring him into his room and get him settled for his nap. It was only five o'clock, but apparently he napped for a half hour after dinner, then played cards or watched television until eight, talking-head shows or sports, and then went to sleep at eight thirty. His father was safe and well cared for and knew Theo loved him. He believed that.

The moment he hit the cold air outside, Theo felt *different*, as if his cells were rearranging themselves. He put his truck keys back in his pocket and took a walk down the path by the river, an idea slowly forming.

Could it be the answer?

The longer he walked, the cold December air rejuvenating him, the more he knew it was.

Theo knew—finally—what he had to do. And he was fully prepared to do it.

Chapter Fifteen

"Oh, that'll work," Lila said, custard cruller midway to her mouth. The MacDougal triplets sat around the kitchen table in Lila and Merry's condo, gobbling up the treats they'd gotten from Coffee Tawk. "Platonic spouses? Merry, please tell her. I can't even with this."

Merry gave Allie a more sympathetic look than was on Lila's face at the moment. "I know you're trying to find a solution, Allie. But living like roommates with a man you're in love with? I don't think you'd survive three days. You'll go out of your mind."

"Right?" Lila said, sipping her mocha latte. "Poor Henry will have his diaper on backward. Ethan will have two diapers on. Olivia three! And Tyler will never get changed at all. Those poor quads. Their mother went off the deep end."

Allie put her cupcake down with a hard sigh. Seriously, she could see all that happening. And she'd probably ruin every meal she attempted to make for her clients. She'd add sugar when it called for salt. Baking soda instead of baking powder. She'd forget to turn the oven on. Actually, she'd done that a few times without having lost her mind.

"But what can I do?" Allie asked. "I can't go through what I did two years ago. I can't be worried sick every night that he might not come home. I have to emotionally distance myself from him."

"First of all," Merry said, pointing her cruller at Allie, "that's never going to happen."

"I'll give the second of all," Lila added. "Even if you did manage that and you lived as housemates, do you really think you wouldn't worry yourself sick about whether he came home or not? So, really, Al, you might as well have the real marriage with sex."

She supposed she hadn't exactly thought out the plan in depth. When he'd told her that he'd been asked to join a task force to go after some dangerous mobster, everything inside her had gone blank. Well, scared and then blank. All she could think was that she couldn't do this, not again. And so pulling away on an emotional level seemed the only way to have him in her life, in the babies' lives, and yet not spontaneously combust.

She wanted Theo to be happy, to be the cop he'd always dreamed of being. A cop like his father had been. He'd never talked to her all that much about his father, not in detail anyway, and she knew that his father had become consumed with hunting down criminals after the loss of his wife, Theo's mother, when he was very young. Theo didn't talk much about that, either; he'd brought it up on an early date when the subject of their families had come up, but she hadn't related his own drive to follow in his father's footsteps to his mom.

Her heart squeezed and tears poked at her eyes. Her husband would not be satisfied as a law enforcement officer if he wasn't out there, chasing leads and suspects.

"Allie?" You okay?" Merry asked.

"Theo said we'd figure it out. But I don't see how."

"Well, maybe look at it another way," Merry said, taking a sip of her coffee. "What happened two years ago was an anomaly, Allie. Unusual, once-in-a-lifetime, terrible circumstances that he found himself in. It's not like that could possibly happen to the same cop twice in one lifetime."

Lila nodded. "I guess if you want the marriage to really work, you have to trust him to find the balance. Do you?"

Allie bit her lip as a very dim light bulb flashed on inside her mind. She had to trust him. It really was that simple.

And she did trust him. She had every reason to. She reached for the locket around her neck and just touched it. Sometimes, when she needed a little faith or strength, it was all she had to do.

"What would I do without you guys?" Allie asked.

"Without us, poor Ethan would be wearing *four* diapers right now," Lila said, taking a big bite of her donut.

The MacDougal sisters laughed and finished gobbling up their treats, the conversation turning to their most recent dates. Merry was "very reluctantly" going on a second date with the divorced dad of the triplets, who'd come to their first date with a two-page list of questions about both triplets and girls. Lila had had the "worst date of her life" two nights ago and was giving up on men.

As they sat and talked and laughed and kept their ears peeled for the quads, still fast asleep for their afternoon naps, Allie was relived to realize that figuring out matters of the heart just didn't come easy. Of course, now she was exactly where she was before Theo had sprung the news on her about the task force—and starting right before Christmas.

When he came home, she had no idea what she was going to say about the future of Mr. and Mrs. Stark.

As Theo drove over to the police station, he went over his plan in his head, hoping the captain would be amenable to it. He brought two large cappuccinos, one for himself, one for his boss, to help.

Coffees in his hands, he rapped on Captain White's door with his knuckes. "Cap, it's Theo. Got a minute?"

"Come on in," Morgan White said.

Theo managed the doorknob without spilling the cappuccinos and stepped in, giving the door a nudge shut with his foot. "Stopped at Coffee Tawk. Want a cappuccino?"

"I always want a cappuccino," the captain said. "So you've got an answer for me about joining the task force early?"

Theo handed over the cup. "I have a *proposal*." He sat down and took a swig of the hot caffeine boost.

Morgan White sat back in his chair, arms behind his head. "I'm listening."

"I feel like I was born for the work I was doing," Theo said. "Hunting down serial killers and mobsters and repeat offenders. But now, with a wife and four babies who need me home at six every night? I can't join the task force. Not after what I put Allie through two years ago. But I do have a plan for how I can be part of the team without being in the field, so to speak."

"What's that?" the captain said, taking a swig of his coffee.

"I'd like to become a strategist for the team," Theo explained. "Work the psychological angles of the criminal mind more than chasing after the bad guy. Study the perp or suspect's profile and come up with solid ways to catch him. To be honest, I think it's what I really do best. I can serve the community, the task forces, the PD, and be what my family needs, too."

"A strategist," Captain White repeated. "I like it, Stark. And you can help train one of the rookies in undercover work and surveillance, too. I think you've come up with a great solution."

Relief settled Theo's shoulders from their scrunched position, his muscles loosening, his heart rate slowing down. And as he and the captain spent the next half hour on a written description of the new role and his responsibilities, he felt as though he'd been given one hell of a Christmas gift.

Now he just had to make sure he hadn't already lost Allie—his true gift.

Allie was up in the attic, looking for the box of Christmas tree decorations that she'd avoided last Christmas, unable to bear looking at the ornaments

Theo had surprised her with on their first holiday as a married couple. He'd had a few of their wedding photos put on hanging hearts and he'd conspired with her sisters to make photo ornaments of her parents on red and white stars. She'd hugged him for a good five minutes when he'd given her those.

Ah, there the box was. She'd forgotten she'd shoved it under an old desktop to avoid seeing it on the rare occasions she'd come up here. Last Christmas, between mourning her late parents and grieving at Theo's loss, she just couldn't handle looking at the box the ornaments were in, let alone putting them on the tree.

She sat down on the dusty floorboards and opened up the box, pulling out an ornament photo of her and Theo kissing right outside the Wedlock Creek Chapel. She smiled at how incredibly happy she and Theo looked. Seven years ago. They'd been so young, just twenty-four, and she'd been so madly in love. She still was.

And mission unexpectedly accomplished. Because there was no way she could have some ridiculous platonic marriage with this man. She loved Theo with all her heart, in every way. She would just have to accept, somehow, that he was a cop and that he'd do his best to keep himself safe for his family.

Except the second she thought it, she knew it would be rough going. Maybe they would just "figure it out," as he'd said. Find a new normal kind of thing.

She glanced at her watch. It was now noon, and Theo should be home any minute. He'd texted her that the morning had gone well and that he had a few stops to make. A few minutes later, she heard the door open, and she took the box and went back down the attic steps.

"Allie?" he called.

"Up here," she said, heading down the main stairs.

The sight of him, in his black leather jacket, his green eyes on her, never failed to send a spark up her spine.

"Babies napping?" he asked, a big shopping bag in his hand.

She nodded. "For about fifteen more minutes or so."

"Just enough time," he said.

She tilted her head. "For what?"

"For me to tell you we don't have to have a platonic marriage."

She smiled. "I already came to my senses about that—with a little help from my sisters and these ornaments."

He put down the bag and came over to her, looking in the box. He pulled out an ornament of them on the chapel steps, Allie in his arms, bouquet that her sister Lila would catch at the reception in her hand. "The happiest day of my life is a tie—this day," he said, pointing at the photo on the ornament. "And the day I returned to Wedlock Creek and saw you again and met my children. You and the quads have to come first."

She reached up a hand to his face. "I know you mean that. And I accept that you're who you are, Theo Stark. Your job is part of you. We'll figure it out as we go along. You know what I realized just now? We're not the same people we were two years ago. We'll both handle things differently."

He took the box from her and set it down on the bottom step, then pulled her into his arms. "I don't know what I did to deserve you, Allie. But there's something you should know."

She looked up at him. "What's that?"

"I already turned down the task force."

She gasped. "Really?"

"Really. When I said just now that you and the babies come first, I meant it. I came up with a proposal to let me serve the team as a strategist instead of being out on the missions, and the captain approved."

"Theo, that's brilliant. And right up your alley. You love strategizing and the psychology of the criminal mind."

He nodded. "And now I can be a cop and serve and protect the community without facing down a mobster's machine gun. There are ways I can help without putting myself in grave danger. I have a family who needs me."

She smiled. "No regrets?"

"How could I have regrets when I have you and those four amazing little creatures upstairs? The five of you turned me into a family man. And I want to be home with my family every night."

She wrapped her arms around him and hugged him tight. "Merry Christmas, Theo."

"Merry Christmas. Our best one ever."

"What's in the bag?" she asked, gesturing at the big shopping bag he'd set down.

"Waaah! Waah! Waah! Waaaaaah!" came four distinct little cries from upstairs.

He laughed. "Perfect timing. I'll show you." He grabbed the bag and she followed up the stairs into the nursery. Four little Starks were standing up in their cribs. Theo reached into the bag and pulled out four impossibly small Santa hats. He placed one on Tyler's head. The baby miraculously stopped whining. "And one for you, Mr. Henry. And one for you, Mr. Ethan, and one for you, Miss Olivia."

Allie laughed. Each hat had *Baby* written across the red brim. She grabbed her phone out of her pocket and snapped photos of the babies in their first Santa hats, then a bunch of Theo holding two, and he took pictures of her holding the other two.

"Oh, wait," Theo said. "I forgot ours." He pulled out two more hats. "This one is yours," he said, showing her the *Mom* on it before settling it on her head. "And this one is mine."

She looked at Theo in his *Dad* Santa hat, her Christmas cup running way over.

This *would* be the best Christmas ever.

On Christmas Eve, the four Starks in their tiny Santa hats, Theo and Allie in their parently ones—and Theo in a Santa suit, minus the beard now—sat in the family room, mounds of gifts and wrapping paper all over the place. They'd both gone a bit overboard, but hey, it was Christmas. Their favorite gift was the set of keys each had given the other to the new house, which they'd closed on the day before. It was officially theirs and they'd be moving in a week.

As he looked over at the quads, crawling on their foam mats, Theo glanced down, then closed his eyes for a moment.

"You okay?" Allie asked, touching his arm.

"I just can't believe this is really my life. A few weeks ago, I was hauling hay and rounding up heads of cattle on a ranch out in the middle of nowhere, playing cards with guys whose last names I didn't even know. I wasn't sure if I'd ever get to see your face again, Allie."

He could see tears mist in her eyes and he leaned forward and kissed her on the forehead.

"And then to get you back and find out I'm a father to them?" he said, shaking his head. "I'm the luckiest guy on earth."

She squeezed his hand and for a few minutes they watched the babies play with their new toys, Tyler banging on the new toy piano, Olivia standing up and plopping down at the puppet theater while Henry stood in the window, being the puppet himself. Ethan was building a tower of foam blocks and knocking them over with glee.

"You know what I don't feel so lucky about?" he said. "The endless packing we have in front of us. And we added a zillion more toys and kiddie stuff to the mix." Did anyone on earth enjoy packing up a house for a move? he really wondered. They should start a business.

Allie laughed. "Right? Luckily, Aunt Lila and Aunt Merry offered to help."

As Allie raced over to stop Ethan from bopping Henry on the head with the new foam bat, Theo thought about the Chadwells, who he'd paid a visit to an hour ago. He'd borrowed the Santa suit from a colleague for the purpose of surprising Hunter with a few gifts, including a gift certificate to a karate dojo in the town they were moving to. Santa had even brought a gift for Snickers, a "skunk" squeaky toy. Hunter had been so surprised he'd burst into tears and hugged Theo ferociously, then he'd ripped open his gifts and thanked him profusely, playing fetch with Snickers and his new toy.

June had let him know they were moving tomorrow and that Hunter was looking forward to the fresh start where he could be the boy who'd make his dad proud.

Theo knew all about that. He'd given both Chadwells a hug goodbye and Snickers a scratch behind an ear, and then he'd driven home, barely able to believe how big his heart felt. The years he'd spent on that cattle ranch, his heart sometimes felt like nothing or shriveled up. Now it was bursting.

Theo's stomach growled as he sniffed the air. Allie had made a huge Christmas dinner, essentially Thanks-giving dinner, since he'd missed that, and it smelled insanely good. She'd invited her sisters, and Virginia Gelman and her husband. Apparently, Allie and Vir-ginia had become quite close recently. Theo had invited the rookie he'd be training in dangerous field surveil-lance—off the field, of course. The captain had let his colleagues know that Theo would be contributing to task forces and operations as their strategy point man, and whenever he ran into one of the officers in town over the past couple of days, they called him Professor. That was A-OK with Theo. Allie seemed to like it, too.

"Oh, before company comes, I have one more Christ-mas surprise for you," he said. He reached for the little velvet box he'd hidden in a bowl under the coffee table.

"Another surprise?" Allie said, her eyes sparkling.

He nodded and got down on one knee in front of her. "Mrs. Stark," he began. He reached for the little velvet box and opened it.

Allie gasped, staring at the diamond ring nestled inside. "Are you proposing, Theo? You do know we're already married."

He leaned over and kissed her. “Yes, but I want us to renew our vows.”

“Renew our vows,” she repeated, her eyes misting up again. “I’m verklempt,” she added, waving her hands in front of her eyes.

He smiled. “Everything about us is new, Allie. So a ceremony to renew our vows seems very fitting, don’t you think?”

“Something new,” she said, a sweet wonder in her voice.

“What?” he asked, tilting his head.

“Just thinking of that old wedding poem. *Something old, something new, something borrowed, something blue.* We’re the old, and the new. You’re the blue, and that crazy Santa costume you’re wearing is the borrowed.”

“Is that a yes?” he asked, pulling her into his arms.

“Dababababada!” Olivia squealed in the background.

“Oh, that is definitely a yes,” she said. “I didn’t think this Christmas could get any more special, but it has.”

He kissed her and held her close. “The first of many.”

Epilogue

Six months later, on a gorgeous Saturday afternoon in Junc, Mr. and Mrs. Stark prepared to renew their vows in the Wedlock Creek Park, their four toddlers as ring bearers and flower girl. The procession would start in a few minutes, and Allie kept stealing glances at Theo, who stood at the other end of the "aisle," on a shiny red carpet Lila had found for the occasion, looking absolutely gorgeous in his tuxedo.

And next to Theo was his best man—his father—looking exceptionally dapper in his own tuxedo and blue tie, to match the bridal dresses. Clinton Stark looked quite happy to be out enjoying the day and the special occasion. Allie knew how much it meant to Theo to have his father as his best man.

All of his colleagues from the WCPD were in attendance as well, including Detective Reed Barelli and all five of his kids, who were impressively well behaved. Allie could see the Gelman Girls, Virginia in a fancy suit like the one Allie had worn for her almost-wedding to Elliot Talley, sitting up toward the front, and several others of Allie's clients were dotted around. And in the middle row of chairs, there himself *was* Elliot Talley, who'd brought his new girlfriend, Hallie—no lie. Lila and Merry could put themselves into hysterics over that one. Hallie was a sweet single mother of one kindergarten-age boy, so hopefully, if they made it to a wedding of their own, Elliot wouldn't go racing away. He'd been very pleased to be invited to the vows renewal, and Allie wished him and his girlfriend all the very best.

As she stood behind the huge potted trees meant to provide a gathering place for the wedding party, she turned her attention to her dear little quads, who were getting a little antsy at all this boring standing around. Tyler, Henry and Ethan wore tiny versions of their father's and grandfather's tuxedos and looked so adorable that Allie couldn't stop taking pictures of them. And Olivia, in her periwinkle dress with the lace hem, dropping rose petals a bit early, was having the time of her life.

"The Aunts MacDougal"—as Theo jokingly referred to them—who were also Allie's co–maids of honor, were in charge of keeping eagle eyes on the little wanderers. Where the Stark quadruplets could run, they charged. And naturally, as a huge white-and-yellow butterfly flew by at toddler eye level, Olivia shouted,

"Butterfly!" with a point and all four Stark toddlers went chasing after it.

Merry dutifully raced off after them, scooping up Henry and then Ethan. Lila, meanwhile, almost ruined her own pretty dress to catch Olivia before she could take a running slide after the butterfly. Grass-stain disaster averted in both cases. Tyler was bribed to follow the group back to the wedding party spot with a promise of two M&Ms, which Aunt Lila handed him from the just-in-case-we-need-bribes stash in her fancy clutch purse.

Allie was thrilled that Merry and Lila had both come with dates. Merry was still dating the divorced father of triplets and Allie wondered if there would be another MacDougal sister wedding in the near future. According to Merry, if she did marry him, she'd have to avoid the Wedlock Creek Chapel like the plague, since adding multiples to triplets would be one too many kids for her. Considering that Allie and Theo were renewing their vows in the *park* for that very reason, Allie totally got it.

Lila's date was a rancher—a first for Lila, who tended toward suits and ties. She refused to say a word about him, so the man, tall, dark and very good-looking, was shrouded in mystery. Allie would just have to get the details out of her later. And since Lila was the queen of asking the most personal questions, she was going to get it given back to her and then some. Allie wanted info. She smiled as Lila snaked her arm around her rancher's arm and then nodded at Merry, who did the same. It was time for the ceremony to begin. For some crazy reason, Allie had butterflies of her own flying around, right in her stomach.

And then Allie heard Lila whisper "Hit it," to her neighbor Geraldine, who was in charge of the music for the occasion, and the wedding march came over the sound system.

Finally, it was Allie's turn to walk down the red carpet. Holding her beautiful bouquet against the off-white lace tea-length dress she'd fallen in love with during a shopping trip to nearby Brewster, Allie started toward her husband and her future, the wedding poem checklist in her head.

Something old: Allie and Theo before.

Something new: Allie and Theo now.

Something borrowed: One of Olivia's little rhinestone-dotted haircombs, which was tucked into the chignon at the back of her head. She felt *très élégant*, even if she were wearing a hair accessory bought in Baby Bonanza.

Something blue: Allie's police sergeant of a husband, not to mention the police presence at the ceremony. True to his word, Theo did come home every night at six, maybe two or three times in the past six months staying late to work on a strategy with the team for capturing a suspect at large. He thrived in his new role and had discovered it tapped into interests he wanted to study more deeply. Theo was the opposite of blue when it came to how he felt about his work.

As Allie approached her husband at the end of the aisle, his father beside him, her sisters beside her, Theo pressed his hand against his heart and mouthed, *You look so beautiful*. She smiled at him, afraid she'd cry and start the raccoon tracks down her cheeks, ruining her makeup. Luckily, though, their "officiant" began talking and Allie focused on him for the moment.

Since this was a reaffirmation of their vows and not a legal ceremony, anyone could "officiate," and Theo had asked his captain to do the honors. Morgan White, in full uniform, spoke about rare second chances and a love to last forever, and then Allie and Theo each read the vows they'd prepared for today.

Finally, the little ring bearers—Ethan holding a tiny pillow with Theo's ring, Henry holding a little pillow with Allie's ring, and Tyler between them, linking arms with both—were coaxed up; and Theo snatched the rings before any of the boys could fling the bands off the pillows and into the grass, never to be found again, or at least not for a half hour of looking.

With her gaze on her handsome husband, Allie slid the ring, engraved with *Forever, Allie* onto his finger. And then with his gaze on her, he slid her ring onto her finger.

"Feel free to kiss your hearts out," Captain White said with a smile.

And so they did, Theo dipping his wife to a wolf whistle from someone in the rows of chairs. Lila, probably.

"You it!" Olivia shouted, tapping Ethan as they went running across the grassy area in front of the canopy.

"You!" Ethan said with a giggle as he tapped her back.

"No, *I'm* it," Theo said, mock-chasing his delighted toddlers on the grass.

"Ahhh!" the quads screamed, racing in all directions.

"Got you!" Theo said, scooping up Henry and twirling him around in his little tuxedo before scooping up Ethan.

"And I've got you!" Allie said, plucking up Olivia and Tyler.

Whoa boy, one-and-a-half-year-olds were a lot heavier than babies, she thought, giving them each a smooch on the cheek. Soon enough, she'd barely be able to lift one.

Then the six Starks continued up the aisle together to claps and cheers from their guests, a family forever.

* * * * *

If you loved this story, be on the lookout for Melissa's next book,

A New Leash on Love,

the first book in Furever Yours,
a brand-new Harlequin Special Edition continuity
kicking off in January 2019
about couples finding love—both romantic and pet—
through the Furever Paws Animal Shelter!

And for more adorable multiples, check out these other books in The Wyoming Multiples miniseries:

The Baby Switch
Detective Barelli's Legendary Triplets

Available now from Harlequin Special Edition!

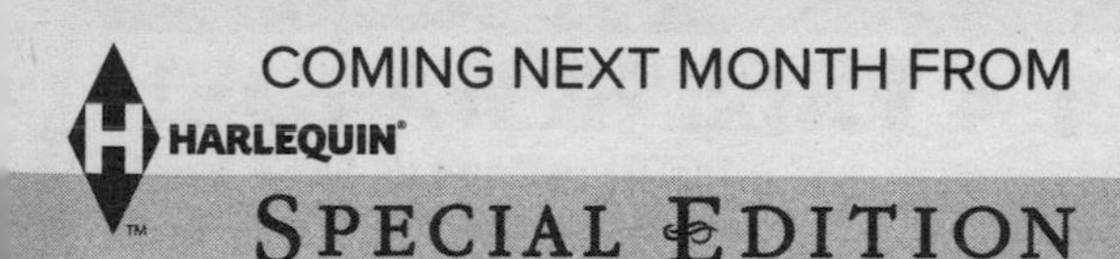

Available November 20, 2018

#2659 BRING ME A MAVERICK FOR CHRISTMAS!

Montana Mavericks: The Lonelyhearts Ranch • by Brenda Harlen

With Christmas right around the corner, grumpy cowboy Bailey Stockton is getting grumpier by the minute. Adorable veterinary technician Serena Langley could be the one to rescue Bailey from his holiday funk. Trouble is, they've got more baggage than Santa's sleigh. But maybe this Christmas, Santa can deliver a happy ending!

#2660 SAME TIME, NEXT CHRISTMAS

The Bravos of Valentine Bay • by Christine Rimmer

Ex-soldier Matthias Bravo likes spending the holidays hunkered down in his remote Oregon cabin. Until Sabra Bond seeks refuge from a winter storm. Now they meet every year for a no-strings Yuletide romance. But Matthias finally knows what he wants—Sabra forever. Is she ready to commit to love every day of the year?

#2661 A RANGER FOR CHRISTMAS

Men of the West • by Stella Bagwell

Arizona park ranger Vivian Hollister is *not* having a holiday fling with Sawyer Whitehorse—no matter how attracted she is to her irresistible new partner. So why is she starting to feel that Sawyer is the one to help carry on her family legacy? A man to have and to hold forever...

#2662 THE FIREFIGHTER'S CHRISTMAS REUNION

American Heroes • by Christy Jeffries

Home for the holidays with her adopted son, Hannah Gregson runs straight into her former flame—fire chief Isaac Jones. Though the pair are determined to keep their distance, Hannah's son worships the brave ex-soldier. If Isaac isn't careful, he just may go from hero to family man by Christmas!

#2663 A DADDY BY CHRISTMAS

Wilde Hearts • by Teri Wilson

Without a bride by his side, billionaire Anders Kent will lose his chance to be a father to his five-year-old niece. Chloe Wilde's not looking for a marriage of convenience, even to someone as captivating as Anders. But sometimes Christmas gifts come in unusual packages...

#2664 FORTUNE'S CHRISTMAS BABY

The Fortunes of Texas • by Tara Taylor Quinn

When Nolan Forte returns to Austin a year after a yuletide romance, he is shocked to learn he is a father. But when he reveals his real name is Nolan Fortune, all bets are off. Lizzie doesn't trust men with money. Maybe some Christmas magic can convince her that she, Nolan and Stella are already rich in what matters!

Arizona park ranger Vivian Hollister is not having a holiday fling with Sawyer Whitehorse—no matter how attracted she is to her irresistible new partner. So why is she starting to feel that Sawyer is the one to help carry on her family legacy? A man to have and to hold forever...

Read on for a sneak preview of
A Ranger for Christmas,
the next book in the Men of the West miniseries
by USA TODAY *bestselling author Stella Bagwell.*

She rose from her seat of slab rock. "We'd probably better be going. We still have one more hiking trail to cover before we hit another set of campgrounds."

While she gathered up her partially eaten lunch, Sawyer left his seat and walked over to the edge of the bluff.

"This is an incredible view," he said. "From this distance, the saguaros look like green needles stuck in a sandpile."

She looked over to see the strong north wind was hitting him in the face and molding his uniform against his muscled body. The sight of his imposing figure etched against the blue sky and desert valley caused her breath to hang in her throat.

She walked over to where he stood, then took a cautious step closer to the ledge in order to peer down at the view directly below.

"I never get tired of it," she admitted. "There are a few Native American ruins not far from here. We'll hike by those before we finish our route."

HSEEXP1118

A hard gust of wind suddenly whipped across the ledge and caused Vivian to sway on her feet. Sawyer swiftly caught her by the arm and pulled her back to his side.

"Careful," he warned. "I wouldn't want you to topple over the edge."

With his hand on her arm and his sturdy body shielding her from the wind, she felt very warm and protected. And for one reckless moment, she wondered how it would feel to slip her arms around his lean waist, to rise up on the tips of her toes and press her mouth to his. Would his lips taste as good as she imagined?

Shaken by the direction of her runaway thoughts, she tried to make light of the moment. "That would be awful," she agreed. "Mort would have to find you another partner."

"Yeah, and she might not be as cute as you."

With a little laugh of disbelief, she stepped away from his side. "Cute? I haven't been called that since I was in high school. I'm beginning to think you're nineteen instead of twenty-nine."

He pulled a playful frown at her. "You prefer your men to be old and somber?"

"I prefer them to keep their minds on their jobs," she said staunchly. "And you are not *my* man."

His laugh was more like a sexy promise.

"Not yet."

Don't miss
A Ranger for Christmas *by Stella Bagwell,*
available December 2018 wherever
Harlequin® Special Edition books and ebooks are sold.

www.Harlequin.com

HSEEXP1118